GHOST
RENDITION

GHOST
RENDITION

GHOST
RENDITION

LARRY WEITZMAN

Humanix Books
www.humanixbooks.com

Humanix Books

GHOST RENDITION
Copyright © 2021 by Larry Weitzman
All rights reserved

Humanix Books, P.O. Box 20989, West Palm Beach, FL 33416, USA
www.humanixbooks.com | info@humanixbooks.com

Humanix Books is a division of Humanix Publishing, LLC. Its trademark,
consisting of the words "Humanix Books," is registered in the Patent and
Trademark Office and in other countries.

ISBN: 9781630061517 (Hardcover)
ISBN: 9781630061524 (E-book)

Printed in the United States of America
10 9 8 7 6 5 4 3 2 1

CHAPTER ONE

I don't like to take kill jobs, but the line between imperative target and imperative payday can get pretty hazy, and my monthly bills are really concrete. Especially since we sent Devon to private school. Paying inflated Westchester property taxes was bad enough, having to pay exorbitant tuition too made me want to shoot someone. And that's not a good frame of mind for a kill job. People who commit crimes of passion get caught. People who get paid to kill learn to stay calm.

Since 9/11 it's been full employment for contractors who can shoot straight. The CIA mandate doesn't allow them to operate domestically, which means hiring contractors. It's still not legal, just harder to get caught. Shaarif Khalid sized up as a typical contract. He was in the country legally. He looked clean. But wiretaps had him planning some nasty stuff. That's what has really changed since The Towers came down. The Agency doesn't wait for the disease to strike. They excise the tumor before it can metastasize.

They love to use medical metaphors. It makes them sound like they're helping people, not killing them. They call me Scalpel, partly because I'm surgically precise in carrying out my jobs, and partly because I dropped out of medical school. That's one of the problems with working for a spy agency—they know too much about you. Like they know I won't kill anybody who isn't a clear-cut "bad guy." They played that up in my brief on Khalid. If I didn't kill him, a lot of other people were going to die. And they knew I needed the money. So, they offered me two jobs: the kill job and a rendition. Renditions are big money, but I had to do the kill job first. They know exactly how to play you.

Two weeks after I got the brief on Khalid, I was in an empty room on the second floor of a nursing home with my Remington Modular Sniper Rifle. There wasn't much time to do my research, and Khalid was pretty cautious. He rode around in a custom Cadillac Escalade with a steel-reinforced chassis. Blowing it up would cause too much collateral damage. It had tinted bulletproof glass, which ruled out an accurate shot even with an armor-piercing round. He lived in a high-security building and was smart enough not to go near the windows.

He had two vulnerabilities—cigarettes and sex. He visited his girlfriend on Wednesday nights when her husband played squash. She was an elegant blonde who spent her husband's money and cheated on him as a thank-you. Would I have been happier if my wife had cheated instead of divorcing me? I had to respect her honesty, but at least I wouldn't be paying alimony.

The bad news was the blonde's building had an underground garage. Khalid didn't have to go outside to get laid. The good news was that he liked a cigarette after. The blonde didn't want her husband smelling smoke in the apartment, and the garage was full of smoke alarms. That meant Khalid lit up outside in the Escalade and opened the window to exhale. He didn't crack it more than two inches, but at under one hundred yards, it was enough to squeeze a shot through.

Everything seemed to go right. Khalid showed up on time and was back out on the street in under an hour. The Escalade window descended, and a plume of smoke escaped. It was the last breath Khalid would ever take. I exhaled as he did and squeezed off a single .338 Lapua Magnum round. I already knew I hit him before I saw his car veer off the road and slam into a light post.

I collected the shell case, stowed my rifle in its unadorned black case, and took the emergency stairs to the ground floor. Dressed in green surgical scrubs, I could have been a visiting doctor checking on one of my patients at the facility. It was like a reflection of what my life might have been.

The lobby security guard was nowhere to be seen, which meant I'd been made. Did Khalid have security that I missed? Even if he did, they shouldn't have been able to make my location off one silenced shot. I didn't have time to figure it out. I knew from scouting that the building had only one working exit. The back doorway was boarded up solid for repair. That would normally have disqualified it as a shoot site, but its sight lines were perfect.

I retreated into the stairwell and stashed my rifle case under the stairs. Sniper rifles are not made for close combat. I hadn't fired my Browning Hi-Power 9 mm in action in almost a year, but I always put in my time at the range.

I had two choices. I could go up or out. Going up and playing hide-and-seek in the nursing home was smarter tactically, but I didn't want a bunch of dead old folks. So it had to be out.

I took off my sneakers, stuffed my socks inside, and tied them together. The lobby was small. The guard's desk to my left was the only cover. That's where my adversary would be. He had likely seen me go back into the stairwell, so he knew I was on him. He would start shooting as soon as I came out. I opened the door and threw my sneakers up into the middle of the room. I didn't expect to fool him, only to draw his eyes. I charged out as I threw and slid on my side with my feet curled behind me and my head angled back. I wanted to give him as little as possible to shoot at. The surgical scrubs gave me a nice smooth slide across the linoleum.

In the time it took for him to shift his eyes from my sneakers all the way down to me on the floor, I hit him twice in the face. He still managed to squeeze off a couple of shots. Hitting a moving target when you have to change your eye level isn't easy, especially when you're under fire. His dispersal of shots was all over the place, but he got lucky. He hit me with one in the chest. The impact from the 9-mm round took my breath away. I wear a level 2 bulletproof vest. It's lighter than the heavy-duty body armor with steel or titanium plates, and it stands up to handguns.

I pulled my scrubs off, dressed my dead adversary, and dragged him to the middle of the lobby. My ribs were on fire. I cracked the door and barked, "Clear!" I didn't know what their code word was, so I garbled it so you couldn't tell what I was saying. I positioned myself behind the desk and waited.

It wasn't long. Two guys came charging in all bright eyed and excited. They couldn't wait to see how dead I was. They both had Remington R51 9-mm. I hit them as soon as they came through the door, one shot apiece in the head.

I went back and collected my rifle. I was wearing gloves and the rifle had no identifying marks, but I felt like Devon used to with his stuffed animals. You know they're not real, but you still can't help getting attached to them.

If I were running this operation, I would have another shooter at elevation to clean up any loose ends. The logical place would be in the building directly across the street. It had a low roof and the clearest line of sight. I slipped my socks and sneakers on and grabbed the bigger of the two guys I'd just hit. He was about a head taller than me, which was lucky. I'd caught him on the left temple, no exit wound. I held him up with my left arm under his armpit, pressed my Browning to his temple, and pushed my way out the door. I angled him in front of me and yelled, "Put down your weapon or your buddy doesn't make it."

It wouldn't fool anyone for long, but holding him in front of me made a shot from across the street pretty difficult. I dragged him to my car, pushed him into the driver's seat, and started it from the passenger side. I spun the steering wheel hard, stamped on the accelerator, and slammed the car into drive.

A series of shots shattered the tinted driver-side window as we whipped around the corner. The tall guy took a hit in the temple less than two inches from where I had hit him. I opened his door and pushed him out as we squared the block. I took his place in the driver's seat and wove through a random pattern of streets to make sure I wasn't being followed. Then I hopped on the West Side Highway and headed home.

On the plus side, I had completed the job, I hadn't left any traceable evidence, and there was no collateral damage. It was borderline miraculous that there hadn't been any passersby on the street. It made me wonder if they had somehow cleared the area. That would mean they had expected me, which didn't make sense. That brought me to the negatives. The whole thing felt wrong. These guys were well armed and well positioned but a little wild. They didn't read like security. And how had they tracked me that quickly? I hated to leave unanswered questions almost as much as I hated to leave dead bodies. They both lead to trouble.

I pulled into my garage, swapped my dummy license plates for my regular ones, and dumped the dummies in a portable compactor. I shredded my scrubs and disassembled my vest. The carrier had been scored so that got shredded. The 9-mm hollow point slug was still in the front plate or I would have had to get rid of that too. They're expensive to replace, but you don't want some cop to get lucky and match fibers from a slug you left behind.

I pried the slug loose and put it in the compactor. I tucked my guns, gloves, and two vest plates in my secure underground cache. I rented a three-bedroom cape across town when Suzanne made it clear that I needed to find other accommodations. It was small, had almost no property and was a little shabby, but the landlord lived in Florida. He wasn't around to snoop, and I convinced him to let me fix up the attached garage in return for cutting my rent. I turned it into my safe room, with reinforced steel walls, deadbolt locks, and an encrypted garage door opener that couldn't be spoofed. I added the safe and the compactor, a dedicated router, webcams, a generator, and enough supplies to withstand a siege. This was a last resort in case my identity got compromised.

The one perk of being divorced is that I didn't have to sneak in after a job. Then again, having to keep secrets from my wife was one of the reasons I got divorced. I made myself a cup of Chinese lavender tea. It calms me after a job and helps me sleep. When I first started, I would stay up all night after a job, and then I'd be wrecked for days.

When my alarm went off the next morning, I was dreaming that I was in the operating room and the patient I was performing surgery on was me. I wanted to go back to sleep, but I had to get ready and take Devon to school. My ex-wife Suzanne was a preschool teacher and was up and out before Devon was. Private schools start later than preschool, which doesn't seem fair with all the tuition I pay.

Luckily, I could make it to the Big House in less than five minutes. It was a hundred-year-old farmhouse Victorian that had been in pretty serious disrepair. We bought it when we first got married and slowly fixed it up. Suzanne was good with home repair. I was good at following instructions. It's no mansion, but compared to the tiny apartment we'd had in Manhattan, it felt huge. And since we had used every dime we had for a down payment, we figured we were sentenced there for life. In old movies, the inmates try to break out of the Big House. I wished I could break back in.

I made a pit stop in the kitchen, then drove the two miles to the Big House at an unsafe speed. My reward was that I got to the front door as Suzanne was coming out. She didn't look that different from when we had first met. She wore her light brown hair short. She hadn't gained any weight, a tribute to the energy it took to chase preschoolers around. And she still had that guileless smile that got right inside me. She gave me a hint of it, then covered it quickly.

"What happened to the Limo?" she asked.

That's what we named my Camry to go with the Big House. It felt like a small victory that she still called it that.

"I left my garage door open and some stupid kids broke in and took my iPod." I still hate lying to her.

"They'll give it back once they hear the awful music you have on it."

"I planned it that way. I don't actually listen to any of it."

Her smile came back out, but then she put it away for good. It upsets her when we get along too well.

"Please make sure Devon takes his lunch," she said.

I wanted to ask why the huge tuition we're paying doesn't buy lunch, but I knew that wouldn't go over well.

"I will clip it to his jacket like we used to with his mittens." I was trying for one more smile, but I knew it was hopeless.

"And Gib, don't forget we have a meeting with his guidance counselor after school. You can't be late for this one," she said and got into her Prius.

She had gone green after the divorce. I still wasn't used to the solar panels on the roof of the house. I watched her drive away, wondering what else had changed. I had heard that she was dating a guy in town, a doctor. I don't think she did it to upset me, but it felt like it.

I walked absently into the house as if I still owned it. Devon came rushing down the stairs. Around town, I was invisible, but he was still willing to acknowledge my existence in private.

"Did you bring it?" he asked.

I reached into my coat and pulled out a Taco Bell bag. I keep a bunch of burritos in my freezer. It was a shameless tactic to buy his affection. Suzanne has the home-field advantage, so I use what I have. "Don't tell your mom."

"She thinks I'm a vegetarian," he said, sticking out his tongue.

"She just wants you to be healthy."

Devon made a farting noise with his outstretched tongue.

"Yeah, meat rules," I agreed.

He gave me a high five, which made me feel guilty. Good, but guilty. I took the healthy lunch Suzanne had made him from the kitchen, stashed it in my coat, and we boarded the Camry.

"What happened to the window?" Devon asked.

"Kids grabbed my iPod."

"With your sucky music on it?"

I laughed loudly and didn't tell him his mother had made the same joke. I let him off on a dead end street around the corner from the middle school. Since he had started seventh grade, he wanted no part of being dropped off by his father in his dirt brown Camry. He gave me his mother's smile as a thank-you. I sat there and held onto it. Then my cell phone buzzed. The text message said one word: "RED".

I slid down in my seat and peered at my side view mirrors. I didn't see anything coming, but RED meant imminent danger. Carrying a weapon when you're not on a job is the easiest way to break your cover. I make one exception. I pulled off my belt, pushed down hard where the buckle meets the leather, and slid the tip of the buckle off. It left a two-pronged piece of metal that looked like the top of a football goalpost. I twisted one prong and bent it at a forty-five-degree angle in toward the other prong, forming a trigger to a palm-sized gun. It shoots a 2-mm caliber bullet at 400 feet per second. A bullet has to go about 330 feet per second to pierce the skin. At close range, my tiny belt buckle gun can kill, but I get only one shot.

Had someone followed me from the Khalid contract? I'd been careful, and even if I had screwed up somehow, why would they wait until the next day to move on me? And what had tipped the Agency to warn me? The explanation that stares you in the face rarely lies. That was what Nachash would say. His voice is in my head way too much. He always said that he never tried to manipulate me, but control the mind and you control the man. That's another one of his sayings.

I opened the car door and slid out into a crouch on the driver's side. If I was wrong, I would probably take a bullet to the head. I hoped they would get rid of my body. I didn't want Devon to have to see his father with his face blown off.

There was a broken, old phone booth three yards up the street that provided the only cover. It was one of those half booths closed on three sides and open on the bottom, but bushes had grown up around it. Devon referred to it as my office. I think he was sort of embarrassed that I work from home, instead of a big office like most of the other dads.

The phone booth was in perfect tactical position if your target stayed in front of you. I slipped around back of the car and exploded out of my crouch into a dead run. Krav Maga does have some locks and submission holds, but Nachash didn't teach them. You shoot to kill, you strike to kill, or you end up killed, was how he taught it. He would not have approved of what I did.

I recognized who was in the phone booth a split second before I hit him. It would have been too late to stop if I had gone for a kill strike or used my buckle gun. I slammed a flat palm into his abdomen just below the ribs into his diaphragm. I heard the air whoosh out of his lungs as he crumpled to the sidewalk.

"What are you doing here, Shrink?" I asked him, knowing that he couldn't summon the breath to answer. "I could have killed you."

Shrink was a human intelligence specialist. It was another medical analogy and a reference to his height. The Agency isn't known for its comedic talents.

I dismantled my belt buckle gun and reassembled my belt to give him time to catch his breath. Devon's lunch had fallen out of my jacket. The organic peanut butter and real fruit jelly sandwich lay face down in the dirt.

"I should have seen you coming. Too long out of the field," he managed to wheeze. He struggled to his feet and got in my car. "New directive. Have to test all field ops. Response time and all that. You did well."

"Bullshit."

"Agency-wide. No choice."

We both knew he was lying. Contractors don't get tested by their contacts. We're not supposed to exist. He had signaled code red while I was dropping off Devon. That was a message. He was telling me I was vulnerable. The question was why? I decided to send a message of my own. I drove him to my house. It broke every rule of spy-craft. You never bring work home. But I had to do something that would make my reaction clear.

"You, or anyone else, come near my son again and it won't end in a conversation," I said as he sat on the couch in my living room.

"Do you have any of that lavender tea you always tell me about?" he asked. "I've been dying to try it."

It was a reference to our shared history and a signal that the stakes were dire. This wasn't a threat. It was a warning.

"Sloppy business last night," I said, as I brought him his tea.

He put it down on the coffee table and didn't look at it again. "I've seen worse," he said.

So this wasn't about the kill job. I sat in the beat-up armchair across from him.

"Your rendition is on a tight timeline," he said. "It's a tricky one. Read the file carefully."

He put a thumb drive on the table next to his untouched tea. Normally I would receive all the information about my assignment in an encrypted email. And I always read the file carefully. "It doesn't sound like a lot of fun. Maybe I should pass," I said.

"We both know it's too late for that. I have complete confidence in you," he said and got up to go.

That went without saying too. So why did he say it?

"Do you need a ride?" I asked. I needed more time to question him.

He shook his head. "Devon's getting big. He looks like you," he said.

He coded me at the school, and then he made another reference to Devon. What was he trying to tell me? "We were hoping he would take after his mother," I said.

"We don't usually get what we want," he said. "Take good care of him. He still needs you."

What the hell was he talking about? Of course I would take care of Devon. I watched him walk down the block and get into a tan Ford Taurus. He wasn't supposed to know where I lived, but he not only knew, he had guessed that's where I would take him. That was part of the warning too. Shrink liked to play games, liked to show he was in control, but he wasn't prone to dramatics. Something had seriously alarmed him.

I plugged the thumb drive into my laptop and used my encryption key generator to open file R227855qxuD. The R was for rendition. The D meant deadly force was authorized. Other than that it was just a reference, a number that mapped to a file. A file that said the Agency had uncovered a sleeper tech. In the Cold War days, the Soviets tried to plant sleepers in our spy agencies.

It wasn't easy. They vet those guys pretty hard. Now sleepers are planted in technology companies. If you know the backdoors to the crypto technology they sell, you can hack the servers that use them. And if you can get into the right server, there isn't anything you can't uncover.

My rendition's name was Danny Pratt. According to the file, his identity was pretty tight. He grew up on Long Island, went to MIT, and worked at a tech startup named Advanced Crypto. He lived alone in an apartment in the Village and liked to hang out at the local Starbucks. A CIA plant at Advanced Crypto had implicated him in cyber espionage linked to terrorist operations. His roots were suspected to be Egyptian with ties to Al Qaeda. The job was to extract him and make it look like he picked up and took a job with a gaming company overseas. I would deliver him to a black airfield. He would get flown back to Egypt where a bunch of CIA-trained contractors would use enhanced interrogation techniques on him, and I would go home to collect my fee. Renditions always paid well, but since the McCain-Feinstein amendment banned EIT, the price had doubled. If you got caught, you got hung out to dry as a renegade traitor.

The rest of the file on Pratt described his work and social routines, his Social Security number, date of birth, credit card and bank numbers, and his family, friends, and acquaintances. It was a thin brief and all tied up neatly. Egyptian origin provided a pretext to rendition him there. And the Al Qaeda ties justified extraordinary measures, by the Agency's own internal logic anyway. Extraordinary renditions can go to Syria, Jordan, Morocco, and a number of other countries where holding prisoners indefinitely and using torture isn't a problem. Some of them are worse

than others, but once a rendition goes to Egypt, they're never seen
again. Was this guy really involved in something that dangerous? If
he had been able to hold cover all those years, he could legitimately
be a serious threat. If Shrink hadn't acted strangely, I wouldn't have
thought twice. But he had gone to great lengths to tip me that
something was wrong. Renditions were dangerous enough. This
one came with land mines.

CHAPTER TWO

hoped that on-site research would give me some answers, but first, I had to get rid of my adrenaline and clear my head. A good fight with Nachash was what I needed. He ran a studio that taught Krav Maga to soft, rich suburban dads who wanted to pretend that they weren't soft, rich suburban dads. He didn't teach any of the classes. He was the mystical presence that gave the place the authenticity that pretenders required. But he did train a hand-picked clientele. I had never met any of his other students, but I could guess that they were mostly in the business. Who else would torture themselves to learn to kill efficiently?

The front of the studio looked appropriately Middle Eastern, with Hebrew lettering and images of desert combat. I went around to the back, which was surrounded by a high brick wall, and went down to what looked like a service entrance to the basement. The hidden security cameras, bulletproof glass, and electronically controlled locks told you that it was something else.

He was waiting for me in one of his specially propped workout rooms. This was not about karate GIs and thick mats. Each room was set up to mimic a real-life situation, and you fought in street clothes. This room looked like a Starbucks. It wasn't the first time that a fight room was coincidentally set up to match my brief. Nachash claimed it was because our chi was in harmony. I had other suspicions.

"I got a red code when I was dropping off Devon. What's going on?"

"You know the rules. We leave our work at the door," Nachash responded with infuriating serenity.

He leaned easily with one hand on a wooden chair. Average height, dark ruddy complexion, and regular features, he wouldn't attract your attention if he was sipping a latte at an actual Starbucks, but I knew better, I knew that when he moved, he was like shifting water, every part of him sliding in perfect unison. It also occurred to me, not for the first time, that he was one of the most infuriating people I've ever met.

"This is Devon. It's personal."

"Examine your premise. You assume that I know something about your work and that I am withholding it from you. What does this say about you?"

"That I'm sick of your pseudo-Zen shit and want a straight answer for a change."

"Impatience betrays a lazy mind."

He whipped the chair he was leaning on at my head as if it were a Frisbee. I ducked, rolled under a table, and flipped it on its side to deflect it. I lifted the table and charged Nachash, trying to crush him between the tabletop and the counter. He spun away with ease. We knew each other too well, after years of sparring, to succumb to obvious tactics.

He broke a leg off from the table and hit me in the small of my back. He has a slim build, and his strength still surprises me sometimes. My bulletproof vest absorbed the worst of the blow, or I would have been pissing blood for weeks. I wear a vest on the job, so that's how I spar. It makes me a little slower and less flexible, but it protects some vital organs. By the time I had managed to break off a table leg, Nachash had hit me twice more. He was enjoying himself.

"You would be dying painfully now. I would stand over you and watch the light go from your eyes."

I faked a looping swing with the table leg, reverse pivoted and hit him with the butt end. He deflected the blow with his table leg, which splintered. He released it and chopped down hard in the same motion. My hands went numb. I dropped the table leg and stumbled backward, barely avoiding the palm of his hand as it swept back up toward my nose.

"Your technique suffers from lack of use," he said.

I could've sparred with Nachash 24/7, and he would have still told me that I don't practice enough. Now though, he happened to be right. I hadn't been to the studio in almost a week. It's amazing how fast you lose your edge. I backpedaled as he launched a series of straight kicks at my groin. He slowly shook his head, which was worse than his insults. He doesn't believe in trying to move away from attacks. The idea is to block them. "The body can't move as fast as the hand or foot," he says. All that jumping around looks great in tournaments and movies, but trying to jump to the side in time to avoid a blow coming straight at your nose is pretty hard in real life. That's the whole point of Krav Maga. The Israelis invented it to be the ultimate in street fighting. It isn't fancy. You block your opponent's strike and then launch a strike of your own in the same motion. "Turn defense into offense," is another Nachash favorite.

I stumbled and fell to my knees. His kick took me in the chest. I leaned into it before it could gather full force, jamming his foot back toward his leg. My ribs were still sore from the bullet I took.

The vest dulled the impact, but it still brought tears to my eyes. I locked his leg with my right hand and brought my left fist up into his groin. It wasn't my best punch, but it must have hurt plenty.

Nachash barely flinched. Everyone gets hit. The best fighters recover the quickest. He broke my hold on his leg with a sharp downward thrust. I whipped my head backward knowing that his next move would be a kick to my head. It still caught me under the chin and sent me flying backward, my legs pinned under me. He kneeled on my chest and gave me the ceremonial punch to the throat.

"You are dead . . . again." It was the way we ended every fight.

"Go ahead, tell me all the things I did wrong," I said, as I lay on the ground.

"You got in one good blow."

It was so close to a compliment that it almost made my ribs stop hurting.

"You must make better use of the geography. What were the weapons at hand? Where do you have the advantage, and how can you get me there? Why am I positioned where I am? Where do I want to move you? Fighting without thinking is fighting to lose."

That was more like it. I started to answer, but he waved me silent and sat down cross-legged next to me.

"You have been distracted lately. Why?"

I struggled into a sitting position. I am not flexible to begin with, and sitting cross-legged with a vest on is not comfortable.

"Family stuff. Nothing you care about."

"I care deeply about family. It is the soil in which our roots grow strong."

"I don't even want to try to figure out what that means."

"You do yourself a disservice by pretending that you are not philosophical."

"You waste your time pretending that I am."

"How old were you when your mother brought you to me?"

This caught me by surprise. Nachash always chided me that looking back meant missing the moment.

"You had just turned ten and you were getting bullied. I asked you what you wanted from me, and you said your father wanted you to learn how to fight. I asked you again what *you* wanted, and you said you wanted to learn so you didn't have to fight. You were philosophical even then."

"I got that from *The Karate Kid.*"

Nachash shook his head.

"Are you trying to tell me to walk away from my assignment?" I asked.

"I never involve myself in your work. Your body and your soul are my only concerns."

"Will this assignment separate my soul from my body?"

Nachash stared back at me. He never laughed at my jokes. I had done a fair amount of research into Nachash's background over the years. It was suspiciously clean. He grew up on a kibbutz in Israel, studied with Imrich Lichtenfeld who founded Krav Maga, and then came to the United States to spread his version of it. He lived in a part of the studio's basement that I had never seen and appeared to have no personal life.

Krav Maga is all about brutal efficiency. It has none of the ceremony of other martial arts. Nachash added back some of the spirituality. Sometimes I thought he was brilliant. Sometimes I thought he was full of shit. I always wondered if he was secretly a recruiter for the Agency.

"I'd love to sit around and laugh it up, but I have to get yelled at by a guidance counselor," I said.

"Your son could use the discipline that I taught you."

"You're very persistent for a Buddhist. Aren't you supposed to practice acceptance?"

"I accept what I cannot change."

"There's no way I'm getting Devon involved in any of this. Not ever," I said more angrily than I intended.

"You will do what you believe is best. Hopefully, you will come to see the truth of what that is."

I left without saying good-bye. The man made me crazier than my ex-wife. I had barely enough time to get my car window replaced at Mike's Service Station in town and still get to Devon's school on time. Mike's a terrible mechanic, but I still use him for the small jobs because he's quick, he takes cash, and he isn't curious.

I got home in time to grab a quick shower. Suzanne kept telling me that I should get one of those low-pressure showerheads that conserve water. A good hot shower is one of the few luxuries I have left. The bathroom filled with steam as I tried to organize my thoughts. Things were moving too quickly. "The slower your thoughts, the quicker your reactions," was another Nachash favorite. I needed to figure out what Shrink was trying to tell me. What did he tell me? What didn't he tell me? Where was the pattern?

I heard the door to the bathroom open and prepared for a different kind of assault. Mimi stepped into the shower and pressed her oversized breasts against me. She was recently divorced and had splurged for a boob job with the settlement. A slim redhead, she had opted for double Ds, which were definitely overkill, but they still felt pretty good sliding against my back.

"I thought we talked about this," I said.

"You wouldn't have given me a key if you didn't want me to use it."

"It was supposed to be for emergencies."

"This *is* an emergency," she said, grinding against me.

I've been trained to resist standard interrogation techniques, but these attacks were rarely standard. They started a couple of months ago. I'd had innumerable talks with Mimi about the impropriety of midday booty calls between neighbors, but it never seemed to stick. Mimi and her husband, Carter, had lived next door before he came out of the closet and divorced her. She had given me an emergency key when I moved in and practically demanded that I reciprocate. It had seemed harmless enough since I never let work come anywhere near my home. The first time she had let herself in, opened her coat, and revealed her heavily augmented figure, I was eating dinner in front of the television. I'd almost thrown my knife at her out of reflex. Having to explain a dead, naked neighbor lying in my living room would have been extremely inconvenient. Mimi had been staging imaginative surprise attacks ever since.

I grabbed her under her thighs, lifted her against the wall, and jammed myself inside her. That's the secret of any well-planned assault, know your enemy's weakness. And Mimi had intuited mine. I had no real social life, and I wasn't ready to live like a monk.

"How did you get so strong?" she gasped.

Mimi had noticed my muscle tone the first time we were together. Luckily, she was more than willing to take post-divorce bodywork as an explanation. The scars were harder to account for. I hinted at a terrible childhood accident that I still didn't like to talk about. Getting naked with someone who knows you is dangerous to your cover. That's one of the reasons I kept telling Mimi that we had to stop, but I couldn't seem to convince her.

Mimi climaxed loudly, toweled herself dry and left the bathroom in a swirl of steam. She came, she conquered, and she left. Now I had to hurry if I wasn't going to be late for the guidance counselor. I put on fatherly looking brown slacks and a light blue button-down shirt. They both needed ironing, but I didn't have time, and I suck at it anyway.

The newly replaced window on my Camry didn't exactly match the others, which bugged the hell out of me. I rationalized that it would probably get shot out again soon anyway. Tinted windows are expensive to replace, but they make it much tougher to get an accurate shot at the driver. I would have gone for bulletproof, but it's visibly thicker, which is hard to explain when you're carpooling kids to a bowling party. And it's very expensive. Some contractors keep separate cars for their jobs, but then you have to worry about where to keep them and who might see you driving off in a different car. My ten-year-old mud brown Toyota Camry hides nicely in plain sight.

I parked in a handicap spot, sprinted to the main office and was told by a condescending secretary that the guidance office was on the other side of the school. More sprinting, sweating, and heavy breathing, and I burst into the guidance office. There were three closed doors. The nameplates read Ms. Trank, Ms. Persky, and Ms. Costello. I couldn't remember which one was Devon's guidance counselor. I knocked on Ms. Trank's door and was greeted by a short, pit bull of a woman who informed me that she had never heard of Devon Alexander. I knocked on Ms. Persky's door next and got an even less pleasant surprise. Suzanne was seated across the desk from Ms. Persky and next to her was her boyfriend, Dr. Dean Rowan. They both turned on me with accusing looks as if I were the intruder.

"Who are you looking for?" Ms. Persky asked.

"I'm Devon Alexander's father," I said.

"I thought you were the father," she said to Rowan.

"I'm definitely the father," I assured her.

I was beginning to think that I was really overpaying for this school.

"I spend a lot of time with the boy, so I wanted to be here to do whatever I can," Rowan said.

Who says, "the boy" and what the hell was he talking about?

"That's my chair and Devon's my kid. You can get up and leave," I said and looked over to Ms. Persky to back me up.

"At least *he* was on time," Suzanne said.

"He's still thirteen years late to be Devon's father and the job is filled."

"It's okay, Suz, I'll wait in the car. I don't want to cause any problems. This is supposed to be about Dev," Rowan said, finally vacating the chair.

I wanted to hit him in the windpipe so badly my hands twitched. Suz? Dev? It was clear provocation. It didn't help that the guy was taller than I was, wore more expensive clothes, and had those big brown eyes that are perfect for making fake trust-worthy expressions. I had never hurt anyone who wasn't part of a job, but I was seriously contemplating an exception.

"Thanks, hon," Suzanne said, and squeezed his hand.

I felt like she was squeezing my stomach. I know Ms. Persky talked to us for a while, but I couldn't take it in. I kept hearing Rowan saying, "Suz" and "Dev" like they were his family, not mine. Then I was outside the school and Suzanne was the one who was mad.

"Why did you have to make a scene? Dean was just there to be supportive. He and Dev spend a lot of time together now."

"Dev? Who the fuck calls him Dev?" She hates when I curse.

"At least he had a clue Devon was getting into trouble," she said.

"What kind of trouble? Devon's a great kid."

"He's not handing in his homework. He spends all his time locked in his room with his computer doing God knows what. He's having problems."

"This tight-ass school is the problem. We should put him back in public school, and he'll be fine," I said.

"We got him into this school because he was having problems. You can't pretend they don't exist."

"I'm not pretending anything. I'm just not freaking out because he likes to play computer games and he's a little bit of a wiseass." I knew as soon as I said it that I would regret it.

"Oh, this is me freaking out. Freaking out that you get to drop in and be the good guy, and I'm the one who has to nag him about his homework. Freaking out that you spend one-tenth of the time with him that I do, but somehow you're better qualified to know when there's a problem. Freaking out that I try to make sure he's healthy and safe and reasonably happy, and you get to toss it all in the garbage and give him Taco Bell and lie to my face about it. That's me freaking out."

I could have pointed out that she was, in fact, freaking out, but I didn't think that would help, and I had to admit that she probably had a point. Devon's a quirky kid. He's a lot like I was at that age, and I didn't have an easy time of it. That's how I ended up with Nachash. But that wasn't what I wanted for Devon.

Suzanne began to cry. I wanted to hug her and comfort her, to tell her that we would figure it out, that Devon would be fine. I moved toward her, and then Rowan had her in his arms. I was lost in my own thoughts and never heard him coming. In other circumstances that could get me killed. This felt worse.

"I'm sorry," I said and walked to my car.

I hoped that Suzanne watched me go, but I couldn't bear to look back. The Camry's new window rattled at me the whole drive home.

CHAPTER THREE

I dressed in dark blue jeans, a black t-shirt, and white canvas sneakers I bought to blend in downtown. And I didn't have any clean laundry, so buying fresh clothes was a bonus. I packed my surveillance gear into a backpack and drove into the City. I had wanted to do a little more background first, but I needed action. I cranked up the radio and tried to stay out of my head. I made good time and found a parking spot on the street. I get paid in unmarked cash. It's not like I can expense parking fees.

My rendition, Danny Pratt, lived on the top floor of a five-story walk-up, no doorman. It took me under five seconds to pick the lock on the front door and another five to get into his apartment. I scanned the living room and kitchenette before finding his router in his bedroom. I pulled a silver key chain out of my backpack. I squeezed it gently on the top and a plug popped out. I plugged it into one of the router's LAN slots and squeezed again, which inserted a tiny chip into the router. It would let me monitor any computer that connected to it. The apartment had four electrical outlets. I replaced their covers with ones that included tiny webcams. The apartment was small enough that they wouldn't leave dead spots. I was in and out and back on the street in fifteen minutes.

Starbucks was next. The brief said Pratt stopped here every day after work. Either lax security was part of his cover, or he was overconfident. I bought a Grande Americano, found a seat in the back corner, and took out the *New York Times*. I planted a tiny webcam under the table. Its wide-angle lens took in most of the room.

Ten minutes later, I left and set up two doors down at Peter's Pub. I ordered a club soda, opened my newspaper, and slipped on my glasses. They had a transmitter that took in the feed from the webcam. All I had to do was look up and to the right to view it. It picked up audio too, but I didn't bother to put in my earpiece. With all the ambient noise, I wouldn't be able to get anything useful.

Pratt strolled in a little after five, ordered some kind of too sweet latte and took a table by the window. I guess writing cryptography algorithms has good hours.

I knew he was twenty-five, but he looked like he was barely shaving. He wore a starched white shirt with gold cuff links and a purple jacket. He had a bright green scarf wrapped around his neck and a green backpack slung over his shoulder. Green boot-cut jeans and purple high tops completed the outfit. It was like he was on the way to a costume party, but I couldn't figure out who he was trying to be.

I sipped my soda and watched Pratt bang away at a paper-thin laptop. As soon as he went home and connected to his router, I would get a look at what he was doing. Until then, it was a boring watch-and-wait.

I was down to the end of my soda, and the bartender had started to give me dirty looks, when two short, squat guys wearing European cut black suits walked in. The Suits sat to Pratt's right with their backs to the wall. Black suits weren't all that rare in this neighborhood anymore, but these weren't imports, they had been bought in Europe. The shoes had too. Middle Eastern agents love to shop in Italy. It's an easy tell, but they can't seem to stop. And these two looked like they were eyeballing my guy.

I was trying to decide whether they posed a threat to the operation when another guy sauntered in dressed like I was except with a pair of Ray-Bans. The only reason I made him was that he practically did a sitcom double take at the Suits before he sat at a table on the opposite side of Pratt. The Suits saw it too, and they looked as confused as I was. The only one who was oblivious was Pratt.

This was the second time in three days that I had unexpected company. It couldn't be a coincidence, not after Shrink's warning. I was not going to step into a shitstorm like this blind. I was going to go home and signal Shrink and demand some answers, or I was going to walk. I knew bailing on the job would end my career as a contractor, but it was better than ending my life. Then the shooting started.

The Suits headed for Pratt's table. Ray-Bans got up to intercept them, stopped and looked like he was about to burst a blood vessel trying to figure out what to do. The Suits ignored him. They were about to grab Pratt when Ray-Bans pulled out an SR1911 Commander and started firing. It's a good accurate gun for close combat, but he didn't hit anything but ceiling, like he was trying to warn the Suits. They pulled out matching Desert Eagle .50 calibers, which are huge. They were designed by the Israeli military, and if they hit you, there isn't much left. The Suits weren't interested in warnings. They blew up Ray-Bans like he was a cheap piñata. The whole place went crazy. Everybody ran around bumping into each other trying to get out. Pratt calmly closed up his laptop, put it in his backpack, and got up to go with the Suits.

I had my stuff stowed and was out the door before Ray-Bans hit the floor. I didn't have my vest on. I usually don't wear it for routine research surveillance. But I charged ahead anyway. I know that saving Pratt from a pair of Middle Eastern operatives to rendition him to another group of them didn't make much sense. But he had the look of a little boy who found himself in a mess yet was sure he would get off with a warning. He reminded me of Devon. I knew Shrink had probably planted that idea, but I still couldn't help it.

The Suits waded through the swarming crowd with Pratt between them. They were headed for the back exit. If I tried to push my way in against the tide, I'd be right in their sights. I shot out the glass in the front window instead, leaped through, and got behind a table for cover. I could still see them through the webcam. The Suit on Pratt's right turned and fired. The other one kept moving with Pratt. They were obviously well trained and had worked together for a while. The .50 caliber rounds splintered the table. I rolled to my right and pulled another table in front of me. The Suit looked over at his partner to see if he was out the door. Normally it would have been a safe move. I was behind the table, and he only glanced for a second. He didn't know I could see him. I popped up and hit him square in the face. My 9-mm slugs weren't as big as his .50 calibers, but this was one of those times when size didn't matter. He was dead before he hit the floor.

His partner didn't look back. How many years had they worked together? How many times had they escaped situations like this? He pulled Pratt to his side to make sure I couldn't get a clean shot and kept moving. I picked up the table and ran at him like I had with Nachash. The Suit stopped, pinned Pratt with one hand, and aimed with the other.

"Danny, fall down," I yelled.

I didn't know if Pratt would have the presence of mind to do it, but he let his legs go limp as if we'd practiced. The Suit's shots went high, and I slammed the table into his face. He went limp too. I hit him across the temple with the butt of my Browning to make sure. Pratt got to his feet and followed me out like a puppy that was happy to be taken for a walk.

I got him into my car and made for the West Side Highway, looking hard for anyone following. If my brain hadn't been turning before, now it was cranking. A routine research surveillance had turned into a public shootout, complete with dead bodies and civilian witnesses. That was usually enough to get you retired even if it wasn't your fault. The good news was that there weren't any security cameras, and it was complete bedlam by the time I showed up which meant I wasn't likely to be identified. The bad news was that I had grabbed my rendition over a week before the earliest possible drop-off date. That meant he was my problem until I could dump him.

I sent Shrink the same code-red message that he had sent me, but this one was real. It went to a series of burners he carried and required an immediate response. I got nothing. I sent it again and still nothing. Shrink was my single point of contact. I didn't know anyone else and no one else knew me.

"Who were all those guys?" Pratt asked.

I had almost forgotten he was there. "You need to be quiet and enjoy the fact that you're not dead."

"Where are we going?'

It was a good question. Shrink had safe houses set up in the South Bronx, but his lack of response could mean they were compromised.

"Wrap your scarf around your face like a blindfold. Make sure you can't see, or I'll have to take your eyes out." It was always a good motivator. People are sensitive about their eyes.

"Slump down in your seat and don't talk until I tell you to."

It took me forty-five minutes to get home in rush-hour traffic. I was violating the cardinal rule again, but it was all I could come up with. I tightened Pratt's blindfold and sat him on the floor against the built-in workbench in my garage. It was left over from the prior resident. Suzanne had kept most of the tools we had bought, since she was the one who knew how to use them. I had picked up enough from her to build a decent hiding place for my work gear. I pulled Pratt's hands behind his back and secured them to the leg of the workbench with plastic ties.

"You don't have to tie me up. I promise I won't go anywhere," Pratt said.

"We don't know each other that well."

"Can I at least have a drink? I like orange soda if you have any."

I found a bottle of Dr. Pepper Devon had left in my fridge. I filled a plastic cup and held it for him. Part of me was amused by the kid, and part of me wanted to shoot him.

"Dr. Pepper is not as good as orange, but it's an underrated beverage," he said.

I heard the phone ringing. "Don't make too much noise and I'll get you some more," I said to Pratt and gagged him with a bandana.

I let the answering machine pick up. "Hey Gib. You there? It's Connor. You going to pick up the phone or what? You better be writing. Call me back, you Bozo."

Connor called everyone Bozo. He made a bunch of money with a line of books "For Morons." They're like the "For Dummies" series but dumbed down even further and full of crude jokes that Connor himself came up with. I've been one of his most successful writers. As it turns out there's a large group of men who like books about violent topics and don't mind being called morons. The books weren't exactly Shakespeare, but the pay was decent and the hours were flexible. I used a pen name, only Connor knew that I wrote them, and he thought that I was just a nerdy weapons nut. My first book, *Sniper Rifles for Morons* was his top seller, and he was expecting big things from *Stabbing Weapons for Morons*. I was late on my next chapter, but he was going to have to wait.

I put on my vest and got back in the car. Shrink didn't live far from me. His real name was Robert Brooks Jr. I wasn't supposed to know that, just like he wasn't supposed to know anything about me, but that's the business, you try to keep secrets, and you try to uncover them.

He and his wife and two kids had a house across the county right on the water. It made me wonder how much guys like him got paid. He got to sit in his backyard and gaze out at the water while I was out getting shot at. Maybe it was time I asked for a raise.

I saw the flames as soon as I rounded the corner of his block. The entire house was engulfed. I only got a glimpse of the damage as I drove by. I didn't want to attract attention. I could see that someone very good with incendiaries had gone to work on his house. It didn't look like there had been a big primary explosion, more like a bunch of smaller fires started in strategic locations. I heard the sirens of incoming fire engines in the distance. I thought about checking for survivors, but I could tell from my quick look that nothing was left.

I tried to make sense of what I had seen as I made my way through the local roads back to the highway. I couldn't believe someone had gotten to Rob. He once let slip that he knew my father named me after John Heysham Gibbons, a famous surgeon. My dad wasn't subtle. He was an orthopedic surgeon, and he wanted me to be one. He thought Dr. Gibbons Alexander would be a distinguished name. The joke ended up on him. I'm not a doctor and everyone calls me Gib, which my dad hates. Rob told me that he understood how I felt. It drove him crazy that everyone in his family called him Junior. He said it made him more driven. He wanted to prove that he wasn't junior to anyone. He thought that if my dad hadn't named me Gibbons I might not have dropped out of med school. I told him it was because I didn't have the hands to be a surgeon and everything else seemed like second place. He said that was exactly his point. He was a pain in the ass like that, but I had sort of considered him a friend. Maybe that was an illusion that he had fostered to control me. I didn't know, and I didn't care. I just hoped he was alive somehow. But if he had escaped, why hadn't he answered my red code?

I was almost at Nachash's studio before I fully realized where I was going. I was closer to the attack this time. And they didn't mess around with fire. This was high explosives detonated in the studio, enough to bring the whole thing down. There was still smoke rising from the ruins when I got there. I should have driven away, but I couldn't leave knowing that there was any chance Nachash could be trapped in there. The odds were remote, but I had to know.

I drove to the back parking lot and went for the stairs, but there was nothing left. I ran around to the front and picked my way through the rubble of the studio. I could see that the floor had collapsed down all the way into the basement. Anything or anyone down there was pulp. I always thought of Nachash as a cross between a superhero, a shaman, and a Jewish mother. He couldn't die. He was a force of nature. I had an emergency number for him that I had never used. I called it and got no answer.

I stood there, looking around like an amateur, as if I was going to spot the bad guys running away. The fact was, the bad guys had likely planted the bombs hours ago and used a timer or remote detonator. They had gone after Rob and Nachash in rapid succession. I ran for my car, dialed Suzanne, and tried to sound calm when she answered.

"Is everything okay?" I said.

"I'm still mad at you if that's what you mean," she answered.

"Where's Devon? He didn't go over to my house or anything did he?"

"It's not your day to have him, and I don't like upsetting his routine."

"I'm not asking for him to come over. I just want to know where he is."

"In his room alone with his computer. That's the problem, in case you haven't been paying attention. That's where he spends all his time."

"Okay, I won't be in my house for a while. You guys shouldn't visit until I'm back."

"What are you talking about? Where are you going?"

"Nowhere, just business."

"What kind of business?"

"I have a call on the other line. I'll call you soon. Kiss Devon for me."

I hung up before I could say anything else stupid. I was supposed to be a trained liar, and I was babbling like a kid in the headmaster's office. Even if they had located me, they weren't likely to blow my house until they knew I was in it. If I played it right, I might be able to smoke them out.

I pulled over to the side and called up the home monitoring app on my phone. It controlled a series of webcams strategically placed inside the house and around the property. I had installed them myself. I was better with electronics than with home improvements. I had done the same at the Big House. Suzanne didn't know, of course. I tried not to use them to spy on her and Devon, but it was hard not to peek once in a while. I checked both houses and saw nothing unusual.

I got back on the road, checking to see if I was being followed. I spotted a red Porsche, three cars in back of me. At first it was a vague feeling. A brightly colored luxury car was not the usual choice to follow someone, but you get an intuition when you've done this long enough. I moved into the right lane and turned my blinker on. He followed. I killed my blinker and swerved back into the center lane like I was lost. He followed again.

I kept up the lost routine, made a big show of looking down at my phone like I was figuring out where to go. At the last minute, I swerved from the center lane off the parkway and onto the service road. I cut over to the shoulder and braked hard. I pulled out my Browning and rested it in my lap. The guy in the Porsche followed me off the exit at high speed. I cranked down my window and hit his back tires as he went by. He lost control as the tires blew and careened off the road about twenty yards ahead of me. I pulled up behind him and jumped out of my car with my Browning drawn. It was a reckless move, but I could see his front airbag had deployed, and I was counting on his being shaken from the crash. I made it to his passenger side window while he was still trying to pull his gun loose from the airbag pressing against his shoulder harness. I shot out the window and yanked the door open.

"Put both hands behind your head and look at me."

He hesitated. I shot out the window behind him. That got his attention. The gun he had tried to pull was an SR1911 Commander like Ray-Bans at Starbucks. It didn't necessarily mean anything, but it was an interesting coincidence.

"Who are you working for?"

He shook his head. I brushed the glass off the seat and slumped down next to him. The cops were likely to show up soon. I had to get him somewhere I could question him. I was googling a list of possible motels when a rain of bullets took him. They were 9-mm hollow points, aimed from a passing Mercedes with tinted windows. I don't know if they were aimed at him or me or both. They sprayed the car and kept going.

I ran back to my car and pursued. They weaved in and out of traffic with a heavy foot on the accelerator. They didn't read like pros. Their shooting was high volume and inaccurate, and their driving was something out of a bad gangster movie.

I pulled into the center lane and kept them in sight. The Camry wasn't exactly a sports car, but I'd had some subtle enhancements done, including souping up the engine in ways that I don't understand. I'm not much good with cars. I know that it accelerates quickly. Straight-ahead speed is nice, but acceleration is more important.

They veered from the left lane to the exit and almost caused a pileup, but I was ready for it. I slowed down as I hit the exit, and sure enough they had pulled over to the side and tried the same trick I had. I needed to come up with something new if these jokers were onto it.

I braked hard, popped open the door, and ducked behind it, my Browning in hand, but they were on the move again before I could get off a shot. Their tires screeched as they pulled off the shoulder, spun, and headed back up the exit against traffic. They sent another spray of bullets my way, for the fun of it. All they hit was gravel. I would almost have laughed except a piece of gravel put a big spider crack in the window I'd just replaced.

I heard police sirens in the distance. The last thing I needed was to get tied up with a bunch of local cops. I turned for home instead. My head was spinning. How many separate groups was I dealing with? Who was trying to kill who? And why were they all driving nicer cars than I was? The one thing I knew was that it somehow tied to Pratt. I resisted the urge to speed on the way home. Getting pulled over when you are carrying is never a good idea. And my guns don't show up on any registries. By the time I reached my neighborhood, I was buzzing with questions. Pratt better have some good answers, or neither of us was going to be very happy.

I parked around the corner and picked my way through the hedges into Mimi's backyard. If someone was watching my house, I needed a good vantage point to spot them. The webcams at my house had limited range. I let myself in and crept up the stairs hoping Mimi wasn't home.

She came out of her bedroom holding a glass of wine and wearing a silk robe that she didn't bother to close. She smiled triumphantly as if she had been waiting for me to finally show up. She had been a lawyer before she got married, and now she spent the afternoon drinking. Then again, maybe Mimi was the smart one. If I could spend my afternoon in my robe instead of getting shot at, I would gladly make the trade.

I slipped past her and looked out her bedroom window. I didn't see any flashes of light from a tree or rooftop.

"Checking to see if any of the neighbors are watching? Don't worry; our secret is safe. Unless you like being watched."

Mimi slid off her robe and undid my pants. I took care of my belt. I didn't want to end up shooting off one of her expensive breasts.

"Aren't we in a rush," she said.

I wasn't in the mood, but it would have taken too long to extricate myself. I hoisted her up against the window and gave it my best while doing another visual sweep of the street. I rolled Mimi onto the bed when we were done and she laughed hysterically, pointing to the heart shaped impression her ass had made on the window.

I kissed her forehead and got dressed.

"Please come again," she said, which started another laughing fit.

I took a pit stop in her bathroom and surveyed the street facing the back of my house. No signs of surveillance. I checked my home monitoring app again to make sure that no one had gotten inside. I started with the garage. I didn't see anything suspicious. I also didn't see Pratt.

CHAPTER FOUR

I had no idea how they had found my house, but I assumed they had taken Pratt and left someone behind to clean me up. I checked my other webcams and almost did a double take. Pratt was sitting on my living room couch, drinking Dr. Pepper from the bottle, and typing away on his computer. I pulled the Camry into the garage and went into the house with my Browning out. Pratt didn't blink.

"Who cut you loose?" I said.

"I did."

He pressed a cuff link and it sprouted a serrated, half-inch blade. "They were a gift. I love spy stuff. I wanted to be out in the field like you, but I can't shoot. Or fight. And I get asthma if I run too much."

"Does your outfit come with any more tricks? Maybe Batman's utility belt?"

"What do you mean outfit?" he asked.

"What you're wearing. Your costume."

"These are my clothes. Nerds don't wear pocket protectors and thick glasses anymore. We're cool now."

"Right." I did a quick check of the house to make absolutely sure it was clean. Pratt kept working like he was hanging out at Starbucks. I sat down across from him in my beat-up old easy chair. It was one of the few things I got in the divorce, and that was because Suzanne hated it. I put my Browning on my lap and waited for him to stop typing.

"Sorry. I had to make sure they couldn't track us here," he said, finally putting his computer aside. "I got to all the traffic cameras and satellites. It wasn't hard, but it took a while."

"Who are 'they'?"

"The people who tried to take me, who else?"

"You're going to need to start from the beginning and don't leave anything out. If I shoot you, I'll probably have to throw out the couch."

"Why would you kill me after you saved me?"

"I get cranky when I don't know who's shooting at me."

"Okay, ever since I started developing Tiresias I knew I was being watched. They named it for a character in Greek mythology who was blinded for revealing the secrets of the gods. Ironic, right?"

He looked at me like I should get the joke. I didn't.

"Anyway, it turned out that they had someone on the team watching us. It was that hot. I know that the NSA is paranoid, but after all the background checks and stuff, I didn't think they'd be that obsessive. That's ironic too, huh?"

I waved my hand for him to get back to the story.

"At first, it was kind of cool. I don't usually like to work in teams. I did most of the work, but a couple of the guys were sort of helpful, and they were funny."

I pictured the world's nerdiest fraternity. "What happened with you and your funny friends?" I asked, hoping the point to the story was somewhere in sight, but there was no hurrying him.

"The code we were writing was elegant. I felt like we were creating something beautiful. Then I started to think about what it was supposed to do. I mean the whole point of spying is getting information, I get that, but this was different, right?"

"Pretend I don't know a thing."

"The idea is for it to send a subsonic signal through TV, radio, IP, whatever, which gets picked up by a computer's microphone and uses the computer's speech recognition software—Alexa, Siri, anything that converts speech to text—to inject a script. Then the script spiders the file directory doing a pretty sophisticated semantic search for anything relevant and beams it back on the same signal frequency. It all goes into a massive database, and the analysts have a field day. The concept is relatively simple, but the execution is incredibly complex."

I didn't understand most of the details, but I got the basic idea of what they were up to. If you're connected to the internet or any other network the spy agencies can get access to, and they can get access to all of them, they can crack your computer like it has a big welcome sign on it. The safest networks or individual computers have air gaps. They are not connected to any outside network. We call them black boxes. They are the last safe places to put sensitive information, and they drive the agencies crazy. Now it sounded like they finally had come up with a way in. If the Agency thought this kid was a foreign agent trying to get his hands on that kind of tech, it was no wonder they wanted him renditioned.

"So Advanced Crypto is an NSA shell working on breaking the black box?" I said.

I could see Pratt tense up. Something about my question spooked him. Then I heard movement from the front of the house.

I had my Browning in my hand and aimed at the door's glass window in one motion. Connor's fat face was pressed against the glass.

"Go into my bedroom and don't make a sound," I told Pratt.

"How did you know he was there?" Pratt asked.

"That's one of the things they teach you at contractor school, you can't depend only on your eyes. Now go!"

He slinked away like a disappointed kid who wanted to stay up with the grown-ups. "There's not actually a contractor school, right?"

I waved him into the room, slid my Browning under the easy-chair cushion, and answered the door.

"Why don't you answer my calls, you bozo?" Connor demanded, pushing his way into the house.

"Connor, it's not a great time . . ." I said, trying to herd him back toward the door.

"Did I see you waving a gun around? You're supposed to be working on stabbing weapons. You're not moonlighting on me are you?"

"You're the only moron I work for," I assured him. "I was doing research on how to use a throwing knife against an opponent with a gun."

"I like it," he bellowed. He looked around suspiciously. "Who were you practicing with?"

"I hired a research assistant. He went out for coffee."

"Great, I can't wait to meet him," he said plopping himself down on the easy chair with the Browning under the cushion.

If he wiggled his big butt just right, he could probably get it shot off.

I heard a car go by and tried not to flinch. Pratt had said something about making sure we couldn't be tracked. I needed to find

out what he meant. It would be too easy for someone to drive up
with a trunk full of explosives.

"I don't want to be rude, but I'm on a roll. I don't want to miss
my deadline," I said, taking Connor by the arm and pulling him
up out of the chair. It was no easy feat, with Connor tipping in at
a quarter of a ton of deadweight. The Moron books must be doing
well, because he certainly wasn't missing any meals.

"I have to take a piss and then I'll get out of your way," he said.

He was in and out of the bathroom quickly and managed to
peek into my bedroom before I could stop him. I held my breath
and thought of how I was going to explain why my research assistant was hiding in my bedroom. Connor looked disappointed as he
shuffled toward the front door. Pratt must have been alert enough
to hide.

"Let's get a beer some time. You can bring your assistant,"
Connor bellowed.

I pretty much shoved him out the door.

"And pick up my calls, you bozo!"

I locked the door and walked slowly to the bedroom. I figured Connor was probably still peering in through the window. I
needed to tell Pratt to stay out of sight. The problem was that Pratt
was gone. I forced myself to walk slowly to the garage. The Camry
was gone too. I didn't have to look at the webcam footage to know
that Pratt must have put it in neutral and pushed it out to the
street before he drove it away to make it sound like a passing car. I
was starting to regret not letting the Suits take him.

I microwaved a burrito and tried to think things through. Pratt
was working on the cyber espionage holy grail, penetrating the
black box. The NSA figured him for a foreign agent and called in

the CIA to rendition him. Most of the spy agencies don't work very well together, but the NSA and CIA have mutual interests. The NSA digs up information like where the bad guys are, and the CIA takes them out with drones if they're overseas or with guys like me if they're domestic. It would make sense for the NSA to have the Agency take care of one of its problems. But it still didn't explain why Rob and Nachash got hit. And why did Pratt think I was there to save him?

I already regretted eating the burrito. My doctor had just told me that my cholesterol was too high, and burritos are little pipe bombs of meat and dairy. It would be a cruel joke if I survived the war I had evidently walked into and then dropped dead of a heart attack. My chest started to hurt just thinking about it. That's another reason I dropped out of medical school. I'm a bit of a hypochondriac. Every med student thinks they have every disease they study, but I actually got symptoms. We'd learn about some nasty rash and I'd start breaking out. I dated a nurse for a while pretty much only because she could get me all the creams and ointments I needed.

I did my breathing exercises to clear my head. I wanted to go out and hunt for Rob and Nachash, but I knew that didn't make sense. Even if the explosions were a diversion and they were being held hostage somewhere, I had no way to find them. The mission priority was to find out what else Pratt knew. That was the way to start to unravel this thing. I had a tracker on my Camry so it wouldn't be hard to find him. I pulled up the app and did a double take. He was on the West Side Highway and by the looks of it, was headed for home. This kid was officially the dumbest genius I'd ever met.

I had to get to him quickly before someone else did, which meant I needed a car. I armed myself and sprinted over to the Big House. Rowan's Jaguar was parked out front. I hoped it was compensation for deficiencies in his anatomy. It's hard to hotwire the newer cars, with keyless ignitions, and I'm a terrible mechanic. Which is why I got myself a signal emulator for my birthday. It looks like a key fob and it cycles through the spectrum of wireless signals until it hits the one to turn the car on. This was the first time I got to use it. It took under a minute to get Rowan's Jag going. I made record time into the Village. I almost wanted a cop to try to pull me over. I could let him see the license plate, outrun him, and stick Rowan with the ticket.

I double-parked across the street from Pratt's apartment just in time to catch him coming out of the building. The Suit was headed up the block right for him, and Pratt was completely oblivious. I had almost no chance of hitting the Suit before he got to Pratt. I knew he wanted Danny alive or he would have shot him at the Starbucks. Yelling, "Danny, get down!" was the best I could come up with. It had worked before, and I wanted Pratt on the ground to keep the Suit from grabbing him and taking cover behind him. Pratt hit the ground and the Suit fired at me.

I ducked behind Rowan's Jaguar. The Suit didn't have an angle on me, but I could tell he was pissed because he kept firing. I did kill his partner, so I didn't blame him. And he put a few holes in Rowan's Jag, which was fun.

I returned fire to make the Suit take cover. He squatted behind a black Escalade. The Suit couldn't get to Pratt without giving me an angle to hit him. And Pratt couldn't get to me without the Suit grabbing him. I could wait him out, but I didn't know if he had reinforcements and I knew that I didn't.

Pratt had parked my Camry right in front of his apartment building. It was a foot and a half from the curb and the nose was pointed out into traffic. I was surprised it hadn't gotten sideswiped. It gave me an idea.

I slithered into the driver's seat of the Jag. Then I hit my Camry's remote and unlocked its doors. It made that annoying beeping sound and flashed the lights. The Suit sent a couple of shots in that direction by reflex. While his head was turned, I gunned the motor and drove the Jag right at him. He turned and fired, but I had already pushed open the door and rolled out onto the sidewalk. The Jag rammed into the Escalade and sent the Suit flying.

"Get in the car, Danny," I yelled.

He was already on his feet. The kid was hard to figure. He was naïve enough to believe he could get away with going back to his apartment, but quick enough to pick up what I was trying to do faster than the Suit had. Pratt already had the Camry started as I dove into the passenger's seat.

Pratt banged the car in front getting out of his bad parking job. I slammed my foot down on top of his to get us accelerating down the street. The Suit yelled, "Chara," and shattered the Camry's back windshield with one of the heavy 12.7-mm slugs from his Desert Eagle, probably out of spite. My poor car was taking a beating. My only solace was that I had probably totaled Rowan's car.

I knew the Desert Eagle was designed by the Israeli military. That alone was not enough to convince me that the Suit was Israeli. Hearing him yell "chara" did. Buddhists aren't supposed to curse, but I'd heard Nachash say it enough to know that chara means "shit" in Hebrew. I can curse in at least ten languages myself, but this sounded like it was from the heart. He was likely Mossad. The question was why an Israeli operative would be after Pratt.

"Are we going home?" Pratt asked as if we were roommates.

"Get on the West Side Highway heading north."

I needed to get him alone. I didn't want to hurt the kid, but I was tired of guessing what was going on. The problem was, I still didn't have a safe house I could trust, and I didn't want him back at my house.

"Can we stop for an orange soda? I get dehydrated when I'm nervous."

I was deciding which wiseass answer to give him when a spray of bullets shattered one of the Camry's few remaining windows. My friends in the Mercedes were back. These guys loved to shoot and didn't seem all that particular about what they hit. They were a car's length behind and to the left of us. They had actually done us a favor giving us a noisy alert that they were coming.

"Get into the left lane. I'll take care of them if they come up on the right."

Pratt almost bounced us off the concrete abutment making the lane change. I threw a couple of shots through the shattered back window to get a feel for what we were dealing with. They deflected off the Mercedes' front windshield, confirming my guess that it was bulletproof. I would have to go for the tires when they made their move to flank us on the right. But they stayed on our tail and didn't squeeze off their usual hail of bullets. That was the real giveaway.

I jumped up in my seat and covered my window with the back of my vest. There was only one reason that they wouldn't try to out-position us, they had a second car. My ribs were still tender, and the bullets hitting my vest felt like they were scraping the skin off them. If they'd had a rifle I would have fared much worse, but the second car was another Mercedes and the bullets were more 9-mm hollow points. Whoever outfitted these guys must have bought in bulk.

Both cars opened up on us, and the remaining windows on my poor Camry bid a sad farewell. I pushed Pratt down in his seat. The body of the car was reinforced with high-grade steel. As long as we stayed below the window line, we were well shielded. But it wouldn't be long before our friends figured that out and went for our tires.

"Switch places with me," I barked.

I slid under Pratt, and for a moment he was perched on my lap like he was my kid and I was teaching him to drive. I took the wheel, swerved into the left lane, and hit the gas. Shards of the ruined front windshield glass blew back at me. This was going to cost a lot to fix, and it wasn't like I could put in an insurance claim. The Camry was souped up enough to outdistance the Mercedes on an open road, which would have been fun. Leaving luxury cars in my family sedan's dust is always worth a smile. But there was too much traffic for that, and I definitely wasn't going to be able to outgun them. That left outsmarting them.

I swerved into the center lane and eased down on the brake, letting the car in front of me put some distance between us. I needed room to maneuver. One Mercedes took the left lane and one took the right lane. When they tried to flank me, I alternated speeding up and slowing down to keep them from getting a clean shot. I didn't vary the pattern. They both caught on at the same moment. I slowed down and they slowed down with me, one on each side. They were so proud of themselves, they each let loose a torrent of bullets. I hit the gas and went from thirty to sixty in about two seconds. Pratt laughed happily as the two cars lit each other up.

"Are you having a good time?"

"You told me I should enjoy being alive," he said.

"I was being sarcastic."

"Oh. I'm not good with sarcasm."

"I'll try to stick with irony," I said.

"That was sarcastic, right?"

I didn't have time to answer. Our friends in the Mercedes had only done superficial damage to their cars, and now they were pissed. They fired at us from both sides, finally figuring out that they should go for the tires. If we got a blowout at this speed, it wouldn't be pretty. This crew seemed less worried than the others about taking Pratt alive, or maybe they didn't mind getting damaged goods. I swerved as unpredictably as I could, but they were bound to get lucky by sheer volume of fire.

"What's our next move?" Pratt asked.

"I have no idea."

"Is that sarcastic?"

I gave him a quick glare and went back to swerving.

"Do you want me to get rid of them?" Pratt asked.

"Not bad, but your delivery needs work."

"I'm not being sarcastic," he said and whipped out his computer. "Those expensive cars almost all have some kind of accident avoidance system. I should be able to get in via satellite through their navigation system."

"Do it fast," I said as a bullet grazed the Camry's back left tire. It wasn't a full blowout. I was able to keep control, but sharp maneuvers were out. The Mercedes on our right darted in front of us. The one on the left accelerated next to us. The back window slid down enough to reveal the barrel of a Remington R51. He was going to blow the rest of our tires, and there was nothing I could do about it.

I gripped the wheel tightly. I doubted I would be able to hold her, but I could try to avoid flipping over. I had my Browning in my right hand, pressed against the wheel. I didn't want to have my gun trapped in my shoulder harness when the air bags deployed. I braced myself for impact. But the Mercedes to our left slammed on its brakes. The car behind it rammed into it, and they both careened into the middle of the highway, causing a nasty pileup. Pratt gave a triumphant war cry.

"Get the other one before he catches on," I said.

Pratt worked his keyboard like a virtuoso pianist. The Mercedes in front of us swerved left and smashed into the abutment.

"I'm not sure what you did, but good job," I said, as we cruised by it.

"That wasn't sarcastic?"

I tousled his hair. He gave me a big sloppy grin. "The newer cars are all big computers on wheels. Once I got in through the NAV, I could access all its systems. Accident avoidance, automated parking, cruise control, oh, I should have made them do figure eights. That would have been cool!"

I pulled off the highway to change the tire. Pratt didn't get out of the car. He sat there in the passenger seat playing with his computer.

I hate changing tires. First of all, I'm a bit of a germophobe. It was yet another reason that medical school wasn't an ideal fit for me. And kneeling on the highway handling greasy car parts is not my idea of fun. And second, I'm not good at it. My iPhone has more computing power than the first Apollo rocket, and they can't give me a jack that you don't have to pump by hand? Plus, at least one of the lugs always sticks. And those stupid doughnut tires look like they belong on the plastic Big Wheel Devon used to scoot around in. By the time I had it changed, I was pretty cranky.

I pulled out my wig and glasses from the trunk of my car and adjusted them looking in the side view mirror. They made me look like a mad scientist who had rolled out of bed. Pratt started cackling as soon as I got into the car. This from a guy who looked like three different people dressed him and never talked to each other.

"You and the Egyptians are going to have lots of fun together," I said.

"That's sarcastic, right?" he asked hopefully.

The fact was, if he was a sleeper agent, then Egypt was where he was headed, and he deserved it. I cringed realizing that it had become an "if" now. That's why I had saved him, right? I had to make sure he was guilty if I was going to send him to die. Uncertainty is dangerous for contractors. It makes you hesitate, which is not good for your health. That's why you're not supposed to talk to your renditions. You're supposed to trust your brief and focus on execution.

"Execution flows from intention." For a moment I thought it was Pratt saying this. Then I realized it was Nachash whispering in my head. Not only was he distracting me, he was annoying. I wished he were still around so I could yell at him.

"If you want to be helpful, stop sounding like a fortune cookie," I replied in my head.

Not only was he still talking in riddles, but I couldn't blame him. Some part of my own brain was making this shit up. I pulled over in front of a bodega.

"You can go inside and see if they have orange soda, but other than that you stay right here. I won't be long, okay?"

Pratt nodded. I gave him his computer back and motioned for him to get out. "If I have to track you down, it won't be pleasant. Not to mention if one of the parade of psychopaths finds you first."

Mike's Service Station was passable for little stuff, but for major repairs I used a glorified chop shop on Jerome Avenue in the South Bronx not far from Yankee Stadium. Lino, the owner, did good work and he didn't ask questions. I hedged my bets by disguising myself as an undercover cop complete with badge and bad attitude. I left Pratt behind because I didn't want to take the chance that someone canvassed body shops looking for us and Lino decided to be helpful. I also wanted to test Pratt. I had placed a tracking microdot on his computer. It would still be a pain in the ass to track him down if he ran, but if he stayed it would tell me something about him.

I dropped off the car, faked a laugh at Lino's wisecrack about my driving, and jogged back to where I left Pratt. While I ran, I tried Nachash's emergency number again. No answer. Then I checked the job boards on my phone. It was the fail-safe Rob and I used. If there was no other way he could safely contact me, he posted a listing on Health Matters, a job board for health professionals. It was very old school, except in the old days you put the ad in a newspaper. The listing would be for a clinical supervisor at the Intelligent Mental Health Clinic—a special person needed for a special mission and a cell phone number. We'd never had to use it, but if Rob had escaped somehow, it was still a possibility. I knew it was a long shot, but I still felt disappointed when it wasn't there.

I started fantasizing about shooting Rowan to make myself feel better. I wouldn't kill him right away. I'd shoot him in the foot first and let him bleed for a while. Then a kneecap. Then one in the gut. A gut shot is a bad way to die. It takes a long time, and it hurts. I considered adding a shot in the groin, but it felt a little cliché. Then I started to visualize him comforting Suzanne outside the school and the groin was right back in play.

When I got back to Pratt, he was sitting cross-legged on the sidewalk, sipping from a can of orange soda with a straw and typing on his computer. What did Rob want me to figure out about this kid? Was he trying to tell me he was innocent or alerting me that he was more than he seemed to be? How many people were after him? And how did they know about him to begin with? When there were this many questions, it usually meant there was what my college statistics professor called a lurking variable. Nachash had encouraged me to take math classes to sharpen my analytical thinking. I thought I was too analytical for my own good already.

A lurking variable is a factor that influences a result without your realizing it. Let's say you do a study on what causes heart attacks. You look at the data and find that the subjects who were on a diet had fewer heart attacks, and you're all excited. You're going to write the diet book that cures heart attacks. The problem is that gender is a lurking variable. Women diet more frequently. They are also less likely to have heart attacks than men. There goes your diet book. All you've done is yet another study that shows that men's tickers go before women's do. Rob had gone out of his way, maybe lost his life, to warn me that something was different about Pratt. Then all hell breaks loose. What variable was I missing? And why were Nachash and Rob likely dead because of it?

"I'm starving. Can we get some food? I'm in the mood for a veggie burger," Pratt asked.

"You're a vegetarian and you drink that crap?"

"I don't believe in killing animals unnecessarily. Why would you kill something that's completely innocent?"

"Enough of the kid next door act. You infiltrated an NSA shop to steal its tech for a foreign country, and people are killing each other over it. I'm not going to forget that just because you remind me a little of my son."

Tears streamed down Pratt's face. I knew that good actors could cry on command, but this was impressive.

"I never wanted anyone to get hurt."

"Well, that hasn't worked out too well, has it?" I said, already feeling bad for yelling at him.

"I'm not a traitor. After what happened to Snowden, I wanted to make sure everyone knew that."

"Then why did you run when I left you alone in my house?"

"I had to get to my apartment."

"Why?"

"For these."

He pulled out a sheaf of paper and handed it to me. It was mostly computer code, which might as well have been gibberish, but one sheet I understood immediately. It was what looked like an authentic whistleblower complaint. That was the lurking variable. Pratt wasn't a foreign agent. And we were both in even more trouble than I'd thought.

CHAPTER FIVE

"Do you want a burrito?" I asked Pratt.

"Is it vegetarian?"

"Sure."

"Do you have any orange soda?"

"How about a Capri Sun?"

"Awesome, that's my third favorite."

I felt guilty lying to him about the burrito, but he did eat two of them and drank three Capri Suns, which even Devon had outgrown.

"If you knew that Advanced Crypto was an NSA shell company, why did you go to work for them in the first place?" I asked.

"I grew up wanting to be James Bond. I thought spies helped their country. But it turned out to be a lot more complicated."

"Yeah, it's not all Sean Connery and beautiful women."

"Who's Sean Connery?" Pratt asked.

I gave him a hard look to see if he was jerking my chain, but the kid didn't have a sarcastic bone in his body.

"How many people have you killed? You've been doing this a long time. It must be a lot. Doesn't it bother you?" Pratt said.

"How do you know how long I've been in the business?"

"I mean you *are* kind of old. What's the retirement age for agents? Do you pack it in when you're sixty-five because I can't see a sixty-year-old guy running around shooting people."

"I'm not an agent. I'm a contractor. And I'm not that old. Focus. You lodged a whistleblower complaint. What was your plan?"

"I realized that Tiresias wasn't only for spying on the bad guys, it was for spying on everyone. I tried to talk to my supervisor about it, but he literally laughed at me. And not in a nice way."

I would like to have been a fly on the wall for that talk.

"I went to his supervisor, but neither of them seemed to appreciate that. I tried to quit, but they made it clear that wasn't an option. They couldn't finish the code without me. I tried sending emails to the heads of every department in the NSA. It was easier to get the addresses than it should have been. A couple of agents showed up the same day and told me that I better stop making trouble or bad things would happen. That's when I made the whistleblower complaint. What else could I do? I didn't want to end up in Russia like Snowden," Pratt said.

"What are all the other papers about?"

"The rest is critical Tiresias code that I didn't want to risk exposing. It was stupid. I have it all in my head anyway, but I get compulsive sometimes. I kept worrying that I would forget it. I wrote down the key elements. Paper is the best security. No one can hack it. Ironic, right?"

The kid was big on irony, but he was missing the punch line. He had two of the most powerful spy agencies in the world in a bigger panic than if he actually were a foreign agent. He was what scared them the most, a true believer. No wonder they wanted him renditioned. They would make him complete his code and then he would disappear and never be heard from again. It was what they called a ghost rendition. You ceased to exist.

"When I first showed up, you thought the CIA sent me to protect you because you were a whistleblower? You realize that NSA agents intercepted whatever you sent before it got to anyone who would give a shit, right?" I said.

Pratt didn't blink. Sometimes the kid seemed like he was in his own world.

"Okay, how about this. Any idea who all these guys are who are trying to kill you, and me in the bargain?" I asked.

"They're not contractors like you?"

"The agency doesn't assign more than one to a job."

"So what do we do now?"

"Can you still get into the CIA servers without giving away where we are?"

"Of course."

"See if you can pick up anything about a big cleanup. We've left a lot of mess the past few days. If we can find out who knows about it at the Agency, we might get some clues as to who we're dealing with," I said.

"What are you going to do?"

"Go to my kid's soccer game. He spends all his time in his room with his computer. I'm worried he's going to end up like you."

The kid actually guffawed. He might figure out sarcasm yet.

. . . .

AYSO is an evil plot perpetrated on unsuspecting suburban families. It's short for American Youth Soccer Organization, and they sucker the parents with happy rhetoric about the joys of participation and the beautiful lessons learned from the beautiful game. And they bribe the kids with participation trophies. If I didn't know better, I would have thought it was an NSA platform to fish personal information from gullible parents and to spot misfit kids to recruit.

I was never very good at sports, but that didn't stop my father from pushing me out onto the Little League field. He said it taught discipline and teamwork. I swore never to commit the same crime against Devon. But Rowan had evidently been a college soccer player, though playing at Vassar hardly seems to count, and he had lobbied Suzanne to sign Devon up with the evil empire.

The field was a good couple of miles away, and my car was at Lino's. I jogged there at a pretty good clip. I tried Nachash's emergency number along the way. He was big on old school conditioning. He scoffed at treadmills, StairMasters, and elliptical machines. I had a jump rope, a medicine ball, and a chin-up bar. Other than that it was push-ups, sit-ups, and roadwork. The whole idea of driving to a gym so you can run or climb without going anywhere seemed absurd to Nachash. AYSO soccer would have sent him into orbit. By the time I got to the field, the game had started. I have to admit I got a lump in my throat seeing Devon in his little green uniform. Then I saw Rowan in a matching jersey, and I felt like I was going to puke it up. That was why Rowan wanted Devon to play soccer, he wanted to coach.

"You're late as usual," Suzanne said.

"You're talking to me. That's a good sign."

"We're still Devon's parents. He needs both of us."

"He has Rowan. What could go wrong?" I said.

"At least he's trying. I don't see you signing up to coach him."

"And that's a bad thing? Have you met our son?"

"Right, it's better that he stay in his room all day doing who knows what on his computer. Dean has been kicking a ball to him every night. His car was stolen and he's still here coaching."

I tried not to smile at the image of Rowan's Jaguar full of bullet holes and jackknifed up on the curb. "Dean wants an excuse to squeeze into a soccer jersey again and pretend he's an athlete."

I felt pretty good about that line until Suzanne teared up, which immediately ended the argument, with me losing.

"I'm sorry. I'm glad Devon is getting some fresh air." I don't know what that means. My mother used to say it to me. "Why don't you go outside and get some fresh air?" Was there something wrong with the air inside? And if there was, why didn't she do something about it? I'd nod my head and go back to reading. Given how I turned out, maybe fresh air could help Devon. "I know you're worried about him, but he's a great kid. He's not doing drugs. His grades are good. He's taking a little while to adjust, that's all. Middle school is a jungle."

"Now you're patronizing me."

"Is it working?" I asked.

"How am I supposed to deal with you?"

"Suzanne, I love Devon more than anything in the world. I would take a bullet for him and not think twice."

"Dying is easy. Talking to your kid is hard," she said.

"I'll talk to him. I promise." I wanted to kiss the tears off her cheek like I used to when we were first dating. Why was she crying back then? I couldn't remember. That probably wasn't a good sign.

Standing next to her and not holding her hand felt odd. Suzanne was a big hand holder. She liked tactile sensations. Gardening, cooking, fixing things, she enjoyed it all. Her hands weren't beautiful to look at. They were hands that got used, with calluses from countless home improvement projects. I didn't have to worry about squeezing too hard. They were always warm. And they fit perfectly into mine.

I had just left med school when I met her. A fellow resident fixed us up. She had dropped out of interior design school. Maybe that's why our friends fixed us up. They thought two quitters would get along. She told me I wasn't a bad person for not wanting to be a doctor. I assured her that not wanting to decorate rich peoples' homes wasn't a character flaw. And when I walked her home, she slipped her hand into mine. We shared a short but nice good-night kiss, but it was the hand holding that stayed with me. Sometimes we'd go to a movie neither of us wanted to see, just to sit in the dark and hold hands.

I looked over at her hands now. They were by her side, within easy reach. How had they gotten so far away?

I checked the Health Matters job board on my phone to distract myself, but there was still nothing. The more time elapsed without contact from Nachash or Rob, the more likely they were dead.

"You're like a little kid," Suzanne said. "You can't focus for ten minutes."

"What is there to focus on? Devon's on the bench, and I have no idea what's going on."

"You should read *Soccer for Morons*. I'm sure Connor would be happy to give you a copy."

Suzanne didn't like Connor or the books. The idea that her husband wrote books for morons never sat well with her. She had encouraged me to be a writer when we were first dating. She said

I told a good story. She thought writing a novel about my relationship with my father would be therapeutic. I half considered it for a while, but Rob was recruiting me pretty hard. Ridding the world of bad guys seemed easier than mining my personal demons. Writing the Morons books, I managed to disappoint my father and Suzanne.

When Devon finally got into the game, or match, or whatever they call it, he looked completely miserable. Rowan kept yelling at him to move. Devon seemed to have no idea where he wanted him to go. My only consolation was that Suzanne didn't look particularly happy with Rowan's yelling. I know that's petty of me, but I thought I was showing remarkable self-control for not shooting him.

The match finally ended after about a century. Devon played less than five total minutes. The teams formed two lines and each kid shook hands with every other kid, which was a nightmare of germ transmission. Rowan took another eternity giving the team a final pep talk. The guy had a captive audience and he wasn't going to waste it.

"Devon looked good out there," I said to Suzanne.

She snorted, which made me want to kiss her.

Finally, Devon came trotting over. "Hey Dad, what are you doing here?"

That hurt. Had I not been around? I guess we used to spend more time together. I'd take him to the park and push him on the swings, which usually made him nauseous. He has my inner-ear issues. I assumed that he had gotten busier with school and doing all the things that he liked to do while not going outside to get some fresh air. I talked to him or texted with him almost every day, more than I talked to anyone else besides Nachash. Maybe it's different with kids than adults. Maybe it was like dog years, going a day without talking to Devon was like a week for an adult. My dad used to make me go on rounds with him at the hospital. All his patients were way too sick. I hated it. I needed to find something that Devon and I could do that he wouldn't hate.

"I'm here to watch you play," I said.

"Why? I suck."

"I thought you were great. You were really moving."

Devon gave me his mother's snort.

"Wasn't Dev awesome? I'm going to make him a real player," Rowan said.

Devon rolled his eyes, and I made a mental note to contribute to his college fund in gratitude.

"We're going out to the diner to celebrate. You're welcome to come." Rowan invited me to join my own family.

I grunted a "No thank you," and gave Devon a high five. "Text me later, okay?"

I watched them walk away together, the three of them. At least Suzanne and Rowan weren't holding hands. I jogged home. I think better on the move. It was going to take a while to unravel what Pratt had set in motion. The question was, where to headquarter the operation. I didn't want to put my family in danger, but I didn't want to leave them unprotected either. The unwritten rule was that agents and contractors leave each other's families alone, but the people who blew up Rob's house and Nachash's studio obviously weren't concerned with collateral damage.

It would be much easier to hand over Pratt to the first agent or contractor who showed up and wash my hands of it all. But the fact was, even if Pratt was trying to compromise a critical

NSA initiative, he didn't deserve to be tortured and killed for it. It was also true that nobody cared what I thought. Pratt had been designated as a threat that I had been hired to eliminate. If I failed, I became a threat and I had no illusions about how I would be dealt with. And it was not like I had anyone to plead my case to. Officially I didn't exist.

Rob's supervisor would know me, at least by my handle, but I had no idea who that might be. The CIA New York field office had been secretly housed behind a false business front in a nondescript building at 7 World Trade Center. The building was destroyed in the 9/11 attacks. The best intelligence was that Bin Laden hadn't identified it as a target. He got lucky. The CIA did too. They didn't lose a single agent. You have to hand it to them, they know how to evacuate a building. They got all the secret files out, but it took weeks to get back to business as usual. The office got rebuilt, but a more decentralized plan was adopted. Agents like Rob got to basically telecommute. That way, if the office got hit again, a network of agents wouldn't miss a beat. His supervisor might be located at the new field office or he might operate remotely. I had no way of knowing.

I found Pratt right where I had left him, on the couch, banging away at his laptop. He was surrounded by empty Capri Sun packages and assorted crackers and chips I didn't remember I had. Was this what Devon did all afternoon, eat fake food and lose himself in his computer? Would he grow up to be like Pratt, smart but dangerously naïve?

"What have you found?" I asked.

"The CIA had a secure connection directly into the Advanced Crypto servers with minimal internal security. That was one of the ways they tried to help the NSA keep an eye on us. Of course, we encrypted our code to mess with them, and we used the connection to open up a wormhole into their servers. They've locked me out of my Advanced Crypto account, and added a new layer of encryption that I've never seen before. It's not hard to hack into the system itself, the firewall is pretty basic, but they've encoded every piece of data separately with a unique form of encryption for each. It's fascinating. Data object encryption isn't new, but this is a creative approach."

"I'm glad you're having fun, but we have to find the people who are after you before they find us. There has to be a primary server for the CIA New York office. That's your target. My contact's name was Robert Brooks Jr. His code name was Shrink. Find anything you can about him, especially who his supervisor was."

"I'll need more firepower. I can't break this kind of encryption off a laptop."

"Where can you get that?"

"Advanced Crypto."

"You want to go back to your old office?"

"It's the only place I know that has that kind of processing power."

"What is the security like at the office?"

"There isn't any. We're supposed to look like a regular company."

"That means they're good at hiding it. Look for a silent alarm system, webcams, and signal detectors. If you can be ready by tomorrow night, we'll take our chances."

"I'll be ready. I just need supplies."

After a quick stop at the local supermarket to load up on candy and soda, I worked at my computer and Pratt worked at his.

"Did you know that the key to throwing a knife is gauging your distance from your target? Every five steps is about one revolution. If you're throwing blade first, you don't want to be eight steps from your target or you're going to hit him with the handle and just make him mad. Actually you're better off shooting him, instead of intentionally disarming yourself, but this is a book about stabbing weapons." I don't know why I was sharing my work with Pratt. Maybe I was lonelier than I thought.

"What kind of book?" Pratt asked with a mouth full of Starbursts.

"*Stabbing Weapons for Morons*. It's going to be a big seller."

"Do you actually enjoy writing it?"

"I would have to say, no."

"Then why do it?"

"I enjoy eating and paying my rent. I don't enjoy alimony and child support, but I have to pay them too. And if I don't get this chapter to my editor by tomorrow, I don't get my next payment, my ex-wife doesn't get her next check, and it's bad times all around," I said.

"Don't you make enough money as a contractor?"

"Not if I don't deliver on my renditions." That one felt bad as soon as it left my mouth.

"Is it hard to hand over people when you know that they're going to be killed?" Pratt asked.

"The guys who take whatever assignments come their way make good money. At least that's what Rob used to say. I told him I would only take cases where there was a clear bad guy. He used to laugh at me and say we're all bad guys."

"You're like me. You want to do the right thing," he said.

"Most of the time I don't know what that is. But yeah, killing should always be hard. And it should never be about money."

"Well, you didn't do it. That's what counts."

"Not yet," I said.

"You're being sarcastic, right?" he said hopefully.

. . . .

I never pulled an all-nighter in college, but I often stayed up all night to get my Moron chapters done. Pratt worked through the night with me, chugging orange soda and chewing Starbursts like they were tobacco. I emailed my chapter to Connor at noon and crashed for a few hours. Pratt kept going. I got us some bad takeout from China Village, the only Chinese food place in town. When we first moved here from the City, Suzanne and I made fun of anyone who was brave enough to eat there. Now I had it at least once a week. Pratt ate it in big sloppy chopsticks-full.

"Any luck getting to their security?" I asked him.

"I did that last night," he scoffed with a mouth full of noodles.

"So what have you been working on?"

"CIA encryption. It's cool stuff."

"I thought you had to get into Advanced Crypto to break it."

"I do, but the more I work on it, the quicker I'll be able to crack it. And it's fun."

"Aren't you worried someone will realize what you're doing and trace you back here?"

He gave me an, "Oh please" look and kept eating.

"How did you start working for the Agency?" he asked, finally pausing to breathe.

"I decided I didn't want to be a doctor and they were hiring."

"I can't see you in med school."

"Me neither, but my father could," I said.

"My father wanted me to go into the family business. He was all set to send me to business school. He was out of his mind when I got a scholarship to MIT. I was always a math geek."

"I know. I've seen your file."

"What else does it say about me?" he asked.

"That you're an Egyptian sleeper agent, for starters."

"Ha. I've never been out of the country."

"That's what a sleeper agent would say. Get ready, we need to go," I said.

I outfitted myself, and we took the train to Marble Hill and then the subway to Fordham Road. I put on my disguise and walked to Jerome Avenue. Lino was kind of a clown, but he did good work. The Camry looked good as new. I'd even had him put in bulletproof glass. With as much as I was getting shot at, it was cheaper than having to replace the windows again, and if anyone noticed, I'd just say I was paranoid. I was already known as a germophobe, so it wasn't too much of a stretch. I endured Lino's usual wisecracks and picked up Pratt back at the subway station.

"Why did you end up as a contractor instead of an agent?" Suddenly he was full of questions.

"I had a particular profile on my psych evaluation."

Pratt guffawed. You could never tell what the kid would find funny.

"I didn't show up as a psychopath or anything. I had a teacher named Nachash who used to say that I live in my own space. I work better on my own."

"What subject did he teach?"

"He would tell you his subject was life. The parts about hitting people were a byproduct," I said.

"I like working on my own too. And Advanced Crypto lets you bring dogs to work, so that's fun."

It was like talking to a little kid, you never knew if he understood what you were talking about. I had to hand it to him though, he had found and disarmed the Advanced Crypto security system and logged everyone out for what looked like routine maintenance. We waltzed into an empty office. It was all cubicles except for four corner offices. Pratt set up in one that belonged to his project supervisor and had the highest-level systems access. I prowled the office for backup security Pratt might have missed.

Most high-level security systems have built-in redundancy. Pratt had disabled motion detectors, signal detectors, micro-cameras, panic buttons, and a kill switch that could shut down the whole complex. They were all connected providing core system redundancy. The best systems also had external redundancy. It would be something totally separate from the primary system, something an intruder wouldn't notice.

"What am I missing?" I asked Nachash in my head. This was a new and troubling development. Talking to myself was bad enough. Talking to my dead mentor made me question my sanity, especially when he answered me.

"What do *you* think you're missing?" This was a characteristically infuriating Nachash answer.

"Why would I ask if I knew that?"

"Why would you talk to a dead person?"

"Because there's no one else around to ask."

Nachash stared back at me in my mind.

"I could ask Pratt. If there's something hiding in plain sight, he might have noticed it," I said.

Nachash gave me his mystical smile. Did it make me a masochist that my own mind was taunting me?

"Since we're chatting, am I doing the right thing here? I'm supposed to do my job, not question my orders. That's the oath I took when Rob recruited me. I accepted the rendition. Just because I don't like it, doesn't mean I have the right to blow it up."

"You never vowed to surrender your conscience," he said.

"Is that what Rob was trying to tell me with his hints about Devon, that there are more important things than the job? But why would he still give me the rendition? Why not blow it up himself?"

"You are always looking for shortcuts. You don't make a move in a fight solely to gain the result. You make it because it is the right move. Trust your process."

I didn't trust the process. Not anymore. The process had left me with a ruined marriage, a son who was evidently having real troubles, and only two friends, both of whom were probably dead. I hadn't told Rob or Nachash, but I had been seriously mulling getting out of the business before all this. As much as I told myself that I hated to kill, the trail of bodies said otherwise. It was becoming too easy, and that was something I had promised myself would never happen. Of course, I wasn't sure how leaving the job worked. It's not like you can go to human resources, collect your severance, roll over your 401k, and say good-bye. I had a sneaking suspicion that the retirement plan for contractors was six feet of dirt.

"Lose your focus, lose your life," Nachash whispered.

"Yeah, yeah," I said in my head, but I went to check on Pratt anyway. The office where he was working was strictly utilitarian. It had a desk, a computer, and a poster from the first Apple commercial with the authoritarian-looking guy with the weird glasses. The only other item of note was a gold letter opener. Pratt should like that, it was an ironic piece for a spy agency. He didn't seem to notice. He was powering orange soda and Starbursts and banging away at his boss's computer like he was playing a video game.

"Did you find anything?"

"I have a basic algorithm that works. It's pretty cool actually. It adapts to the type of encryption being used. I wish I could show it to my artificial intelligence professor. It uses some bleeding edge machine-learning principles."

"That's great. Did you find anything?" I said.

By the pouty look on his face, Pratt was getting the hang of figuring out when I was being sarcastic.

"The problem with the algorithm is that it has a high level of complexity, which means it works slowly. I have some interesting ideas on how to speed it up. I think that . . ."

"Did you find anything?"

He gave me a long-suffering sigh. "He is not very patient, is he?" Pratt said.

"Only I get to refer to myself in third person."

He laughed hysterically. The lack of sleep and the sugar high were finally catching up to him.

"He thought I was talking to him. He's a silly one."

I moved quickly around the desk and saw who, or rather what, he was talking to. It was a scruffy black Labrador that was seated happily at his feet. I examined his collar. The tiny webcam wasn't hard to spot. I had found the external redundancy. Nachash was right: I had lost my focus and we would be very lucky not to lose our lives.

"We have to go." I said.

"But I ..."

"Right now." I took the letter opener on the way out. I wasn't sure why. Sometimes I do things on instinct, and when I look back later it's like I planned them. Nachash said it was the inner mind. I told him that I went to med school, and there was no inner mind.

CHAPTER SIX

We came out of Pratt's boss's office and were greeted by a storm of bullets. There were multiple shooters from at least two angles. I pulled Pratt and the dog into a cubicle. There were stairs behind us and across the floor. The near one was our best hope, but even if I covered Pratt, there was almost no chance he would make it. And if we stayed here, they would go cubicle to cubicle until they got an angle to kill me and take Pratt. We needed a diversion.

"You know how you got into that car's system remotely?" I said. Pratt nodded. He didn't seem scared, which sort of annoyed me. "Can you get into the webcam in the dog's collar and make it show the output of the webcam on your laptop?"

He found a serial number on the camera, flipped open his laptop, and happily banged away. I could hear the shooters moving up on either side of us.

"You might want to hurry," I suggested to Pratt.

He turned his laptop around and I could see the output from the webcam in a window on his screen. "That's what the dog's webcam is streaming."

I took his laptop and put it on the desk in the cubicle. It took me a few precious seconds to get the angle right. I recorded Pratt and I looking down at the camera.

"I need the dog's collar to stream what I recorded in a loop."

Pratt did some speed typing and nodded.

"Give me a Starburst," I said.

Pratt looked through his stash and handed me a lemon one. We were probably going to die, but he still wanted to make sure he gave me his least favorite Starburst. I opened it and waved it in front of the dog's nose. "You want this boy? Go get it." I tossed it into the cubicle behind us in the direction of the stairs. The dog bounded after it. I covered its move with two bursts of fire. If they were monitoring the dog's webcam, they would see what I had recorded and think we were trying to retreat toward the stairs. I gestured for Pratt to be quiet. He nodded, but still managed to silently open a Starburst and stuff it in his mouth. The kid had some strange skills.

I could hear the dog rooting around the cubicle behind us looking for the Starburst. My plan was that the shooters would converge on the cubicle, assuming we were with the dog. I would hit as many as I could, and we'd make an end run for the stairs before they figured out what happened.

The problem was the dog found the Starburst. As soon as it scarfed it down, it would come back to us to beg for more. I had to move before that happened. "Stay here and don't make a sound until I give the signal. Then make a break for the back stairs," I whispered in Pratt's ear.

"What's the signal?"

"I'll bark," I said.

"What if the dog barks? It would be confusing."

"What do you want the signal to be?"

"Orange soda," he said.

The kid had a one-track mind.

"Be careful," he mouthed to me, as if that were an option.

I went down on my belly and snaked my way laterally to the next cubicle. This was the most dangerous part. I needed to get out of the range of the shooters' peripheral vision. It's tempting to go too quickly. You want to get to safety as fast as possible, but quick movement draws the shooters' eyes. I disciplined myself as Nachash had taught me, moving slowly and smoothly. It felt like forever, but I made it behind the next cubicle without drawing fire.

Now I moved more quickly. The shooters wouldn't see me unless one of them turned their head. Sound was my problem. I moved in a crouch, making each step as light as possible. I am not naturally graceful. Nachash used to call me Big Foot. He worked with me endlessly to move silently. I made it to the cubicle behind one group of shooters. I needed to take both of them without tipping off the other group.

I pulled out the letter opener and felt its balance. It was light, which made it hard to get the rotation right. I gripped it like a javelin instead and tried to throw it straight. It took the nearer of the two shooters in the side of the neck. It was a pretty good throw. I would have to remember to put that in my Morons book. I followed my throw and was on his partner before he knew what happened. I hit him on the top of the head with the butt of my Browning. He crumpled without a sound. The shooter with the letter opener in his neck tried to cry out. I hit him in the nose with the point of my left elbow. He made a gurgling sound as he drowned in his own blood. I eased him quietly to the floor.

Both shooters were carrying R51s like my friends in the Mercedes. They're pretty popular now, but these guys had the same kind of lunatic bravado. I picked up one of their guns, shot at the wall behind me, and screamed into the crook of my elbow like I was hit.

A shooter from the other group scrambled out of his cubicle, gun extended. I shot him in the head. He went down hard. The odds had improved.

If each group had two men, as seemed likely, then there was one left. I could wait him out.

"I have more men on the way. You come out with your gun down, and I'll let you and Pratt live," he yelled.

That was a mistake. He was talking when he should have been moving. He gave away his location. He also gave away that he was the group leader and that he knew Pratt's name but not mine. And he was anxious to finish this. He would probably guess where I was and try to come right at me.

I heard his charge before I saw it. As soon as he entered my field of vision, I squeezed off my shot. But it wasn't him. It was the dog and the bullet sailed over its head. This guy wasn't highly trained, but he wasn't stupid. He knew that the dog would sniff me out. Now he had my position, and I didn't have his.

I knew he would try to press his advantage. He came at me from the side. I heard his footsteps and pivoted, but I was too slow. He was going to rake me with his R51. I had to hope I took it in the vest. Then the lights went out. The darkness made him hesitate. I dove onto my stomach, and he fired over my head.

I thought he had fired from a stationary position, but I hadn't seen the shot dispersal so it was hard to tell. I lay there for a moment, not breathing, trying to figure his position.

I heard him settle back on his heels. He had been up on the balls of his feet when he fired. It was a natural reflex to settle back, but he might as well have painted on a bull's-eye. I fired three times in quick succession. Judging by the timing of his fall, I'm pretty sure the second one did the trick.

I yelled, "Orange soda!" and felt pretty stupid. Pratt turned the lights back on and come out from his cubicle. He had his big sloppy grin on. He'd hacked into the office systems and hit the lights through his computer. "Contractor school. They teach you to use more than your eyes."

"How did you know they weren't trained the same way I was?" I asked.

"You said the Agency never assigns more than one contractor."

It was scary. The kid remembered everything I told him. We made it down the stairs to the lobby. I had Pratt stay in the back while I peeked out the front door. Three gunmen sprinted down the street toward us. They had their guns out, not even bothering to try to conceal them. All three carried SR1911 Commanders like Ray-Bans's at Starbucks and the guy in the Porsche. These weren't the reinforcements the guy from upstairs had lied about. This was a different group of playmates. The pedestrians on the street barely reacted. Maybe they thought it was a movie shoot or something, or maybe that's just New York. I had to believe someone would call 911, which meant we not only had another gunfight on our hands, we probably had inbound police too.

I hit the first one in the head, and the other two took cover. They looked offended, like they couldn't believe I had been rude enough to kill one of them before they could get into position. They strafed the front of the building with no apparent aim or intent. The double-glass front doors shattered into a geometric pattern on the lobby floor.

I had three options and all of them had problems. I could try to slug it out with them at ground level and hope they did something stupid, but I was outgunned. I could go upstairs and try to get them from elevation. Taking the high ground was a huge tactical advantage, but if they had any brains, they'd work their way into the building and hit us from two sides. We'd basically be right back where we started. Or I could give Pratt one of the dead guys' guns and have him spray the shooters from ground level to keep them in place while I went upstairs and picked them off. But these guys had already shown that they were rash. If they charged the door before I got upstairs, Pratt wasn't good enough with a gun to hold them off.

I was weighing my options when I heard the police sirens.

When it comes to how to help Devon with his problems in school, or what to say to Suzanne, or what to make for dinner, I can overthink myself to death. But in the heat of action, I'm decisive. My gut told me that these two maniacs weren't going to be scared off by the cops. They were more likely to rush the building. I was going to send Pratt to hide upstairs. I'd hold off the two shooters until the cops arrived and then try to act like a bystander. They'd question me. I'd ask them to take a piss and then make a run for it. If they found Pratt, he could say he was just an employee who got caught in a bad situation. It was far from ideal, but it was the best we had. Or rather, it was the best we had, until the Angel of Death showed up.

She was blonde and stunning and handled a gun like a cold-blooded killer, the perfect combination of manicure and menace. She walked calmly over to the shooters with her gun palmed at her side. She was dressed in a skimpy tank top and tight black shorts. All they saw were legs and breasts. She flashed them a radiant smile and said something that I couldn't hear. They smiled back at her, and she hit them each between the eyes with a round from her Browning 9 mm. Then she walked casually up to the building like nothing had happened.

"Can you give a girl a lift?" she said. She tucked her gun into her shorts. It was like a magic trick, they were so tight. "The cops are getting close. We don't want to be here to greet them."

I nodded to Pratt, and we went out to meet her. I had my gun out. Chivalry and hormones don't trump survival. I kept it on her, as the three of us walked away quickly but not too quickly. Cops notice when they see people running. There had been plenty of witnesses to the shoot-out, but most people aren't too observant. And if they remembered anyone, it would be the gorgeous blonde, not the two average-looking guys with her.

"My friend likes Starbucks, why don't we sit and chat?" I suggested.

She wasn't Agency. Walking up on shooters wasn't their style. She might have been sent here to kill us, and hitting the other guys was a red herring. Or she could be a new factor altogether.

"A little more distance would be better. You're parked only a few blocks from here."

"You're guessing," I said.

"It's a good guess," she said with that blinding smile. "And I know things about your contact that you need to know. Isn't that worth a ride?"

She knew the right button to push. I took her to the Camry. I wasn't happy about it, but if she knew something about Rob, it was worth it.

"Perfect cover car. What did you do to soup it up?"

"Mostly on the chassis and the acceleration." For the first time I regretted not knowing more about cars. That's what they were for, to impress beautiful women. "I added bulletproof glass. I kind of feel like a wimp."

"Good move. You don't want to check out with your hand on your stick," she said and laughed from her belly, like a guy. She sat up front with me. Pratt seemed happy in the back with his laptop. He was young and single and didn't seem affected by the Angel of Death in the least. I made a mental note to talk to Devon. If this was a glimpse into his future, he needed a heart-to-heart talk in a hurry.

"What shall I call you? I assume real names are out," she said.

"Let's say I'm Doc and he's Sonny."

"Why can't I be Doc?" Pratt asked.

"Because she asked *me*."

"I like Sonny. It suits you."

Pratt practically giggled. Maybe he wasn't as oblivious as he seemed.

"You can call me Caroline. It's my cat's name." She made a claw and meowed at me. I almost drove off the road.

I'm not prone to schoolboy crushes. I barely had any before Suzanne. When I was younger, they seemed too far-fetched. And in med school it was a moot point. When you watch spy movies, it seems like women come with the job. The fact is that the job makes it harder. There are too many obstacles. You don't go to a normal workplace with normal hours where you meet normal people. Letting someone get close endangers your cover. And finding yourself attracted to someone you meet on the job is the most dangerous of all. The safe move was to dump the Angel at the curb and keep going no matter what she knew.

"Have you ever been to Sylvia's?" I asked her.

"Is that your girlfriend's name?" she said.

"It's a soul food restaurant in Harlem. The best," I said.

We took a table in the back, against the wall. She attacked the smothered chicken, collard greens, and mashed potatoes like a pro. Pratt was disappointed that they didn't have orange soda. He opened up his laptop and went to work right at the table.

"I've driven you, and I've fed you, now tell me a story," I said.

"You wouldn't respect me if I were that easy."

"The way you handle a gun, respect isn't your problem."

"What *is* my problem?" she said.

"That's what I'm asking."

She gave me that shiny smile. "You're cute. And you have a lot of people who want to kill you."

"Thanks and I know."

"But you don't know who they are," she said.

"And you do?"

"My job doesn't usually include sharing information, but my contact is dead and I'm on my own," she said.

"You're a contractor? For who?"

"For Shrink. Same as you. He got me a message before they got to him, 'Beware of our own.' He said you were the only one I could trust."

She knew Rob's handle, and I had to admit that did sound like cryptic Rob bullshit. "What is that supposed to mean?"

"Let's say you have two contacts battling for turf. One decides to take out the other. How would he do it?" she said.

"Very carefully," I said.

"He'd trump up treason charges and make the case that after what happened with Snowden it should be taken care of quietly," she said.

Pratt perked up hearing Snowden's name. "They wouldn't make stuff up, would they?" he asked.

"They'd convince themselves it was true," I said. This made sense to Pratt. He went back to his computer. "They'd disappear him. They're good at covering their tracks. No one would be the wiser," I said. "That still doesn't explain the present pig fuck." It actually turned me on to say that to her.

"But what if he got wind of it first. Who would he go to? Who could he trust?" she said.

"His own contractors."

"They'd have to get rid of them first. Take out his protection and he's naked," she said.

It was hard to focus when she was saying words like "naked.' Intra-agency politics were legendary, but contacts contracting for kill jobs on each other was insane. It was a shame. I hate to kill women, especially when they're pretty. I eased my hand onto my Browning. It was a comforting gun. It felt better in my hand than the huge Desert Eagle the Suit used or the slick-looking Remington R51s the Yahoos in the Mercedes used. And suddenly everything she said made perfect sense. The guys who tried to hit me in the nursing home after my kill job were carrying Remington R51s. They weren't with Khalid, the guy I was there to snuff. They were contractors, like she was saying. Their contact had tipped them off that I had a kill job, and they figured they could clean me up when it was over. It made my head swim. "What was the split over?" I asked.

"Him," she pointed to Pratt. "Shrink didn't want him renditioned."

I looked over at Pratt, but he was busy with his favorite toy. "Why?" I asked.

"I don't know."

"Who ordered the rendition to start with?"

"I don't know."

"How did the Israelis get involved?' I asked.

"I didn't know they were."

"That's an interesting story. And there isn't a shred of proof," I said.

"How else could I know your contact's handle unless he gave it to me?"

"You might if you were the one who killed him."

"And I killed all those nice young men to gain your trust?" she asked. "You're even more paranoid than I am," she said.

"You helped us for a reason. What do you want?"

"I want to find the people who got to Shrink, just like you do," she said.

I wanted to believe her, which meant I couldn't trust my judgment. "Let's assume that contractors like us have gone to ground to wait this out. Whoever went after Shrink reached for the B Team. Skilled professionals would have finished us today. These guys ride around in Mercedes and shoot off their R51s like they're auditioning for a Jason Bourne movie. The party boys you took care of, group number two, were probably Russian. Putin would love Pratt's program, and they were all carrying SR1911s. They like to drive red Porsches so they can stand out even more than the stupid Americans. And behind door number three, the Israelis. They read like pros, probably Mossad. They saw the chaos and figure maybe they can sneak in and grab it. Did I miss anything?

"Sounds right to me," she said. "What do we do now?"

"I have him. I have no choice. You get to lay low until this is over and avoid doing anything dumb like coming to the rescue of strangers."

"I told you, I have a debt to pay," she said.

"Professionals don't pay debts. They move on."

"Like you are?"

"Like I said, I have no choice."

"You could leave him on the side of the road and not look back. You're making a choice. I am too," she said.

We did one of those ridiculous stare-downs across the table. If she were a guy, I would have wanted to shoot her. But all I wanted to do was kiss her.

Pratt handed her a cellphone. "This is a burner. I need some time to process the data I got at Advanced Crypto. We'll call you when we know our next move."

"Now Sonny's calling the shots," she said treating him to a high-wattage smile.

It wasn't the worst solution. We could contact her or ditch later, and I wouldn't have to shoot her. "We'll go first. Give us ten to see if we've picked up any followers. If you don't hear from us after that, you're good to go," I said.

"I'll wait for your call. Don't stand me up." She put her hand in the small of my back, leaned in and kissed me on the lips.

I tried to make a graceful exit and not let her see that my legs were wobbly. That's how I used to feel with Suzanne. It was good to feel that again, and it was terrible. Now wasn't the right time, and she wasn't the right person. I almost forgot to check that we weren't being followed.

"Can we trust her?" Pratt said.

"You can't trust anyone, including me," I said.

· · · · · · · · · ·

I put Pratt to bed. He wanted to guzzle orange soda again and work through the night. You can get by on short sleep for a while if you have to, but you don't want to get strung out and start making bad decisions.

As I made myself some lavender tea, I had to sniff back tears. If Caroline's story was true, that meant Rob really was dead. I couldn't say I knew him well, but he had defined my entire career. It was like the world itself had changed. And what about Nachash? Believing that he was dead was simply beyond my imagination, especially since he kept talking to me. But if contractors were working in groups, trying to kill each other, then the pile of bodies was only going to grow.

I fell asleep and dreamed that Rob was trying to tell me something, but he was choking to death and I couldn't save him. I woke up to his screams. They were coming from the bathroom. I ran down the hall, pulled the door open. I found Pratt buck naked, yelling at the top of his lungs. Mimi was naked and laughing at the top of hers. She had ambushed the wrong target.

CHAPTER SEVEN

"Mimi meet Sonny, my new research assistant. He's a little shy." I handed her the robe that lay at her feet. "Did you get shy too?' she asked, donning her robe, but leaving it open.

"I'm on deadline. I'll come by when I can."

"I'm sure you will," she said, and made a slow, dignified exit. You had to hand it to Mimi, she didn't fluster easily.

"Is that your girlfriend?" Pratt was fully clothed now and less panicked.

"Mimi's my neighbor."

"Your neighbor is your girlfriend?"

"My neighbor is my neighbor. Why don't you get to work? You can have Starbursts for breakfast."

Pratt spent the day happily trying to decrypt the information he'd hacked. I banged out a chapter called, "Killing with Scissors," which Connor thought would appeal to women, and then I took a run. When I went by the Big House, Rowan was out front throwing a soccer ball to Devon and imploring him to head it back to him. Didn't this guy ever work? On impulse, I cut through the neighbor's yard and around to the back door.

Suzanne was in the kitchen putting the finishing touches on the night's vegetarian concoction. After she had given up on being an interior designer, she had done a brief stint at culinary school.

She liked the creativity of cooking and all the tactile work of chopping, dicing, and stirring. Ultimately, she found the strict hierarchy of the professional kitchen stifling, but I reaped the benefit of her cooking skills. I felt bad that Devon had to suffer through her vegetarian conversion, which seemed to have sapped her zest for creative cooking. At least Rowan wasn't getting gourmet meals. The table was set and the plates were filled with gruel of varied colors. She seemed to be cooking something that might be dessert gruel. I scratched at the window and she let me in.

"I went for a run and I got an allergy attack. Can I borrow a Benadryl?"

It was a pathetic lie, but it did the trick. Suzanne had a hard time resisting the hurt and the downtrodden. If I hadn't been allergic, we would have had a legion of lost cats, dogs, birds, and other wounded woodland creatures.

"I don't know how you survive on your own. I have this image of you eating three meals out of a microwave and having no clean underwear," she said.

She almost never came inside when she picked up Devon. She said my house was too depressing. The fact was that I didn't mind take-out food, and I bought a lot of extra underwear. I didn't correct her. I liked having her maternal instincts aroused in my direction.

She had always thought of herself as a doer. She was going to be a career woman first and a mom second. But none of the careers she tried were ever a love match, and when we had Devon she was over the moon. We would have had a house full of kids if the problems hadn't started. They weren't out in the open at first, but the fact that we both hedged on adding to our family should probably have been a clear sign. Suzanne became a preschool teacher instead and loved every student as if they were the kids we never had. I wish I had found something that I was half as suited for, preferably that didn't involve killing.

"What Rowan is doing to Devon qualifies as child abuse," I said while palming the two Benadryl and pretending to swallow them.

"Don't start."

"Okay. How are *you* doing?"

She eyed me suspiciously.

"I get it that it hasn't been easy with Devon. And I know how much you take that to heart," I said.

"Because I freak out at the first sign of trouble, right?"

"Because you're a wonderful caring mother," I said.

This actually stunned her into silence. I took the opportunity to give her a kiss on the lips. It was a quick one, but she didn't recoil, which was a pretty big win. It had been a long time. She tasted the same. I wanted to grab her and feel her in my arms, but I didn't press my luck. I did manage to crumple up the Benadryl and drop them in Rowan's food before I left. Hopefully it would make him too sleepy for sex.

"Thanks for your help. You were a life saver," I said.

"You should start carrying them with you," she said, trying to gain back her usual distance.

"Then I wouldn't have an excuse to see you," I replied and made what I hoped was a dashing exit.

I ran hard to burn away the thickness in my chest. Was it only that I took Suzanne by surprise, was that why she let me kiss her, or was there something more?

Desire is the enemy of decision. That's what Nachash would say. Then again, he had never been married. I took a cold shower. It was probably good that Pratt had scared Mimi away, at least for a while. I needed to keep my head straight.

The doorbell rang. I finished dressing quickly. Had Mimi decided to make a frontal assault so soon after her retreat?

Pratt answered the door before I could get there. The kid had no sense. He had a big sloppy grin on his face as he welcomed Caroline into the house.

"What are you doing here?" I said, not completely surprised.

"I didn't like my hotel room. This is much homier."

She was dressed in a tight blouse and jeans and carrying a small suitcase. She looked great, but the right thing to do was shoot her.

"You know this is against the rules," I said.

"There are no rules now. What if they track you here? You're better with me here to help."

"How did you find us?" Pratt asked.

"She put a microdot on my back when she kissed me good-bye. I should have guessed."

"Don't be mad. I missed you," she said.

"It was a problem his knowing where I live, but there was a pretty good chance he was going to die. You're a much bigger problem."

"I promise never to tell anyone. Cross my heart hope not to die," she said.

"Not the kind of security I'm looking for."

She reached into her pants and my Browning was in my hand.

"Easy there, Quick Draw." She pulled out a picture of a dark-haired man and two blonde children. "These are my twins. There is nothing and no one I care about more. I'm going to write where they live on the back of the picture and give it to you."

She picked up a pen and scrawled an address on the back. "Even though I'm sure you're good enough to find them off the picture."

"And the guy?"

"My ex-husband. Him, you can kill," she said.

I took the photo. My only alternative was to kill her and I didn't want to do that. Not yet anyway.

"Am I really going to die?" Pratt asked.

"Not with the Angel of Death with us," I said. Caroline gave me a quizzical look. "That's my pet name for you."

"I like it. I might have t-shirts printed up. By the way my name is Caroline. I made up the bit about the cat."

Nachash whispered that she was playing me. I thought he was probably right. But she knew where I lived. I was better off keeping her close for now. At least that's what I told myself.

"I'm Gib. This is Danny, which you probably already know."

"Nice to meet you boys. Let's get to work," she said.

We sat at the kitchen table. Caroline and I had lavender tea, and Pratt drank orange soda. Caroline peppered him with questions and he talked a mile a minute. Some of it was technical, which Pratt seemed cagey about. Some of it was personal, which he seemed to enjoy. And some of it was tactical, which he answered with wild speculation.

I chased down the picture Caroline had given me. It appeared to check out. I was no Pratt, but I wasn't bad with computers myself, and I had some pretty good tracking programs that could crack basic fake identity setups. It was no guarantee, but according to what I could find, she had two kids and an ex-husband in Ridgewood, New Jersey. It was like some karmic dating service had connected us. And it was exactly the kind of distraction that I didn't need. As she continued to question Pratt, I tried to figure out what she was getting at and not get distracted by picturing her naked. By midnight, I gave up trying to do either.

"I hate to interrupt this almost completely useless conversation, but did you get anything on Rob's supervisor?" I asked Pratt.

"Rob *was* a supervisor."

"He was a contact. You must have pulled the wrong file."

"Robert Brooks Jr. CIA, Human Intelligence division. Promoted to supervisor three weeks ago," Pratt read.

"That's impossible. Supervisors don't run contractors."

"Maybe he held onto us for protection," Caroline said. "We were both with him a long time."

It made some sense. I'm pretty sure I was one of Rob's first contractors. He was pretty young when we started. If Rob thought he was under attack, he would go to people he could trust. Then again, it's not like he had confided in us. He gave us some cryptic hints and handed me the rendition knowing it would blow up. "The more we find out, the more confusing it gets. Are you holding out any other information, preferably something we can use?" I asked Pratt.

"Before he was promoted, he reported to a supervisor named Chandler Westfield. Does that help?"

"You waited all this time to tell us that?"

"You asked me to find his supervisor. He's not his supervisor."

"Did you find an address too?"

"He lives in Scarsdale."

"Okay. I'm glad I asked. We're practically neighbors. I'm going upstairs to sleep now. Tomorrow we're going to break into his house, tie him up, and have a nice friendly conversation with him. If you come across anything interesting before then, like say who exactly is chasing us and how to get them to stop trying to kill us, please let me know."

I knew my sarcasm was wasted on him, but I saw Caroline suppressing a smile, which gave me some small satisfaction.

"You can sleep in Devon's room. It's to the right of the bathroom," I said to her. "Mr. Helpful can sleep on the couch."

Nachash had trained me to fall asleep like turning off a switch. Usually, I did a simple meditation exercise and I was out. But it wasn't easy with Caroline in the next room. My gun was under my pillow, but I had to admit that it was fantasy more than danger that kept me awake. When the door to my bedroom opened, I thought I was imagining it. Caroline was backlit from the light in the hallway. All I could see was blonde hair, a white t-shirt and white panties.

"Your room is the other one," I said.

"Maybe I like this room better."

"If this is you trying to interrogate me, I'm not going to crack," I said.

"Want to bet?" she said and pulled her t-shirt over her head.

Her breasts barely moved. Caroline had to be in her late twenties, but her body had yielded nothing to time or gravity. She wriggled out of her panties with an ease that would have put seasoned strippers to shame. "If you want me to leave, say so," she whispered.

"I want you to leave," I forced myself to say.

She laughed and removed my boxers.

"Please leave," I said.

"You'll have to do better than that," she said and slithered on top of me. She managed to touch every part of her body to mine. Her hands found my shoulder blades and pulled me against her. Her feet hooked around my ankles. Her mouth covered my neck.

"You have to leave," I mumbled one last time.

And then she was rocking up and down, and I was inside her. Her back was arched. My hands were on her breasts. Her eyes never left mine, right up until we climaxed together. And then she was on top of me again, smaller now, tucked against me.

"I told you I wouldn't crack," I gasped.

Now that I was in no hurry to find sleep, it found me.

CHAPTER EIGHT

got up early, called Nachash's emergency number, and checked the Health Matters job board. It was like a superstition at this point. Then I went to pick up Devon. Suzanne was waiting for me at the door. I held up my hands palms out for inspection. "I come Taco Bell–free, ready to take our son healthy and happy to his delightful, reasonably priced school."

"Is that a hickey on your neck?" She eyeballed me like a veteran interrogator.

"Shaving accident. I'm trying out a new electric."

Devon came out, and I flipped him the keys to the Camry. "You can start her up."

He loved to sit in the driver's seat and start the car. I moved close to Suzanne and whispered in her ear. "I'm sorry to disappoint you, but I'm glad you're jealous," I said and pecked her on the lips.

"What did you say to Mom?" Devon asked as I drove him to school.

"I told her you had a girlfriend who's eighteen and smokes unfiltered cigarettes."

"There is so much wrong with you."

"You have no idea."

I parked around the corner from the school as usual. I couldn't help glancing at the phone booth and thinking of Rob.

"Do you need to go check your office?" Devon asked.

I had to be careful around him. He was too observant. He would make a great contractor. The thought made me shudder.

"Are you doing okay?" I said. I had wanted to plan some big father and son outing to have our heart-to-heart but circumstances made that difficult.

"Mom told you that I'm a freak or something?"

"Of course not. We're a little worried that you may be having a tough time at school, that's all."

"Because you stuck me with a bunch of spoiled rich achieve-a-trons? No, I'm having a great time."

"You can go back to public school if you want," I said.

"And go through the whole new kid thing again? I finally have some friends who aren't total jerks. They're nerds, but I am too, right?"

"Why do you say that?"

"Nerd isn't a bad word anymore. Mark Zuckerberg, Sergey and Larry, Jeff Bezos, nerds rule the world. I'm getting good grades, I'm not doing drugs. Tell Mom to chill."

And then he was out of the car and gone. My work instincts told me he was hiding something. His tone had the rushed pace and hint of forced bravado that were both tells. Or was it just adolescence? This wasn't the type of interrogation that I was good at.

Rob's supervisor was going to be a different matter. Caroline and Pratt both insisted on coming. I let them, because I wasn't sure I trusted them out of my sight. I argued with Caroline during the ride about why she refused to wear a bulletproof vest. Her point basically boiled down to that I couldn't understand because I didn't have breasts. It was hard to refute.

I picked the lock on the front door with a pick gun and a torsion wrench. It leaves a clear mark, but it's quicker than the standard tools and I wasn't worried about detection. I was inviting Westfield to come home and he would know that.

The house was a big brooding Tudor. It had five bedrooms, a master suite, three smaller bedrooms that looked like they belonged to boys, and one larger one that looked like it belonged to a girl. The attic had been turned into an office. A quick search turned up household bills and personal financial statements. A laptop computer didn't turn up much more. Pratt checked for encrypted files, but it was clean. We split up and went over the rest of the house, but Westfield didn't seem to take his work home with him, as you would expect.

He made it back from the City or wherever he was in good time. We had finished looking around when he rang the doorbell and let himself in. He announced his presence, making sure we didn't get spooked and shoot him. And he came alone, which meant he was open to talking. He sat down on his living room couch and waited for us to gather. He wore gray slacks and a striped, button-down shirt. He had thinning blonde hair and pale blue eyes. He looked like a corporate executive, a corporate executive who could order an execution as easily as his morning coffee.

"Thanks for coming, Mr. Westfield," I said to him as I sat opposite him in a wingchair.

Pratt sat in an armchair off to one side, and Caroline stood between us, keeping an eye on the door.

"Call me Chan, please. Ordinarily we would never meet, but these are extraordinary circumstances. That's why I'm here in person. I'm hoping we can establish trust," Westfield said.

"I'm hoping you would tell us what the fuck is going on," I said with a flat stare. Quickly shifting tones can subtly shake an adversary. He was unfazed.

"Information is a commodity. What do you have to trade?"

"Let's start with your life," I said.

"I could offer you the same," he said. "But I'll give you something else as a gesture of goodwill. Shrink was assigned this rendition, but decided to sell Pratt to the Russians instead. His lifestyle ran ahead of his income. We know you are innocent in this, but that opinion can change."

"Why would Shrink hand Pratt to me if he didn't want him renditioned?"

"He set you up, I'm afraid. I understand how hard that is to believe. Rob and I were old friends. It broke my heart to find out he was a traitor."

"You were so broken up that you executed him," I said.

"Do you believe we would unleash this kind of carnage on our own soil? With the backlash caused by the Snowden incident, our adversaries have felt emboldened. We don't know which one of them got to Rob, but trust me when I tell you that we will find out."

"Why should we believe you?" Pratt blurted out. "All you care about is making sure that you get your new spy toy. Well, you can't complete the program without me, and I won't finish it, not for you."

We had agreed that I was the only one who would talk, but Pratt couldn't help himself. The stare Westfield gave him did not belong to a corporate executive. It belonged to a reptile eyeing a bug.

"I think you will. It's remarkable what impending death does to your priorities," Westfield said.

"You see, you don't care how many people get killed or how much you trample on peoples' rights. As long as you can dig up your dirty little secrets, you don't care," Pratt said, his voice cracking.

"Secrets aren't dirty. People are dirty. People who place themselves above their country. But we know how to deal with people like you," Westfield said.

"You think you know who we are? You think you know anything about us? You don't know anything. But we know who you are. We know who the dirty one is," Pratt screamed, fully unhinged.

I motioned for Caroline to take Pratt outside. She took him firmly by the arm, and he let her usher him out.

"He is a disturbed young man. How much did Rob tell you about his circumstances?" Westfield said.

"I got my brief."

"You two were close, I know he gave you something more."

He was fishing, but for what?

"I imagine you have a deal in mind. Why don't we get to it?" I said.

"We could have surrounded the house, killed the two of you, and taken Pratt by force, but I prevailed upon my superiors to give you a chance."

"To do what? Hand Pratt over and let you take him apart?" I said.

"Finish your rendition and we'll give you the full retirement package."

"Six feet of dirt?"

"Enough money that you never have to see me or anyone like me ever again. That's the carrot. Your anonymity has been your insurance policy. Now that we have an image of your face, it won't take long to find out everything about you. That's the stick," he said.

"You wanted me to come here. You planted that file for Pratt to find."

"You wouldn't have responded to a formal invitation."

"Westfield isn't your real name. And this isn't your house," I said.

"Only a convenient meeting place. As you saw, Pratt is far too volatile to trust with a project as important as Tiresias."

"He gets renditioned and finishes the program for you or dies trying. You get the program or prove that he couldn't finish it and you hand it to someone else," I said.

"I'm pleased that you understand. I want this to end well for all of us. For the Agency, for you, for your family."

"You're the one who needs to understand. Pratt was right, you're never getting the program, and if you come anywhere near my family, I will make it my life's mission to make sure you die in ways even you can't imagine." Talking and moving without one interrupting the other is harder than it seems. Nachash made me recite Buddhist scripture while jumping out of my chair and attacking him. If I broke rhythm by one syllable I had to start over. It throws people off if you can do it right. I was out of my seat and across the room by the first sentence. My hand was on Westfield's throat by the start of the second. My Browning was in my other hand and pressed to his right eye by the time I was done. No one likes anything pressed to his eye.

"Rob was right. I am the best. And I will wade through a division of your agency stiffs to get to you if I have to."

I could sense his pulse rate rise, but he didn't react visibly. He was good. I made a quick exit. Caroline and Danny were waiting in the car. Caroline pulled out fast and did a good job of weaving through the streets to make sure we weren't followed. I scanned for drones.

"Thank you for not handing me over to him," Pratt said.

"I shouldn't have let him get to me. I should have played for time. Now I have to move my family. What am I going to tell them?" I said.

"You don't have to tell them anything," Pratt said.

"It was a setup. They recorded us when we walked in. With the latest facial recognition software they probably have my address already."

"They used very primitive security on their router. I scrambled their video signal and sent them images of the Three Stooges instead. Those guys always make me laugh," Pratt said.

"You staged that blowup? You wanted to storm out of the room?"

"I figured they were recording us. I needed some time to find out how," he said.

"Our boy isn't as naïve as he seems," Caroline said.

They shared a look that I didn't like. Was I the only room she had visited last night?

"Good job," I told him.

He gave me his big sloppy smile like I had given him a puppy treat. I wasn't sure whether to buy it or not. Nachash used to say that everyone is hiding something. Maybe he was right.

· · · · · · · · · ·

I put the car in the garage, swapped out my license plates, and joined Pratt and Caroline in the kitchen. Pratt had found my stash of Starbursts and was working his way through it. Caroline had made us each a cup of lavender tea.

"What do you think?" Caroline asked. "I don't believe Shrink was a traitor."

"I think you should have tortured him. That's what he wants to do to me," Pratt said.

"I don't know what to believe, but I don't believe him. He should have had a boatload of agents waiting for us. He doesn't want us in custody. And he was probing about Rob. He's worried he told me something valuable."

"Did he?" Caroline asked.

"I don't know. He was signaling something to me, but I'm not sure what," I said.

"Something about me?" Pratt asked.

"Because everything's about you?" Caroline said.

Their banter came much too easily.

"Is Westfield, or whatever his name is, the one Rob went to war with, or did he just come down on the side of whoever Rob's enemy is?" I said.

"That's the question," she agreed.

"He's the one who went after Rob," Pratt said.

"Why do you say that?" I asked him.

"Just a feeling," he said.

"From all your years in the business? I'm going for a run. Try to find out anything you can about Westfield, starting with his real name."

"I'll come with you," Caroline said.

"I need you to babysit. He has a habit of disappearing. Don't open the door or answer the phone." I didn't like leaving her alone with Pratt, but I needed space to think.

"You're not going to sneak off and do something heroic and stupid are you?" she asked.

"Not without you."

I ran hard hoping the endorphins would clear my head. I had thought Pratt was simple to read, but I was starting to change my mind. He'd fooled Westfield. He'd fooled me. And something else, he'd said, "We know who you are. We know who the dirty one is." Who was he referring to? Were he and Caroline a "we" now? Maybe it was just a figure of speech, but it bore watching. I looked up and realized I had run to the Big House. The lights were on. I knocked, hoping that Rowan wasn't there. Suzanne answered the door.

"Don't tell me you're having another allergy attack?"

"Actually I came to talk to Devon."

"What's going on?" she asked, suspiciously.

"You said that I needed to get more involved. Is he home?"

"He's upstairs locked in his room as usual. I don't know if your showing up unannounced is the best way to do this."

Surprising him was exactly what I wanted. People don't lie as well when they don't have time to prepare. I couldn't tell Suzanne that, of course. That was one of our problems, she could always sense that I was holding back. She was the opposite. It was one of the things I had always loved about her. If she was happy, you knew about it. If she was angry, you knew about it. And it was all better than walking on eggshells and wondering, the way my mother tip-toed around my father. He rationed his feelings as if he had only a small supply and he was trying not to run out. Except for disappointment. He was always generous with that. And the irony was that Suzanne ended up accusing me of being emotionally stuck and all that was left in the end was disappointment.

And now it seemed that Devon was struggling and I had completely missed it. At least I was here. I was trying. That's more than I could say for my own father. With him, it was always on his terms or not at all.

"He's my son. Do I need to make an appointment?" I said.

"Go on up. See what kind of greeting you get."

"Don't be jealous. We can spend some quality time too," I said.

She shook her head. I was hoping for a smile, but mock disapproval was okay. When we were fighting, I knew we were okay. At the end, it was like a circuit blew and she shut down. I was worried that after our kiss she was going to shut me out.

I walked quietly up the stairs to Devon's room. I knocked on the door and let myself in. I knew he wouldn't like it, but I wanted to see the look on his face. It was surprise with a dash of guilt. He blanked his computer screen and got up to greet me.

"You're supposed to wait until I tell you to come in," he said.

"Why, were you doing something you weren't supposed to?" I playfully looked around his desk for evidence of wrongdoing. I also attached a tiny webcam to the bottom of his computer monitor that would catch his keystrokes.

"Are you turning into Mom? Or did she send you up to spy on me?"

"She's worried about you. I am too. You know you can tell me anything, right? I'm always on your side."

"There's nothing to tell."

"Okay. Do you want to go to the Dog House? We can split their 'five hot dog, guaranteed to make you sick' special, as many toppings as you want. We'll tell your mom we're going for ice cream," I said.

"I have to get my homework done or she'll be all over me."

"Okay. I'll take a rain check. You know you can call or text me anytime."

"You don't have to worry. I'm not a little boy anymore."

"That's *why* I'm worried," I said.

"He kicked you out?" Suzanne asked, when I got downstairs.

"He said he had homework to do."

"I don't know what he's doing on that computer, but I know it's not homework," she said.

"Have you ever tried to sneak a peek?"

"Are you kidding?" she said.

"Yeah, I guess that wouldn't be fair to him."

"I've tried every password I can come up with."

I couldn't help laughing.

"It's not funny. I'm worried about him. I tried taking away his computer, he just used his phone. I took that away and he went to the computer lab after school or a friend's house. I don't want to lock him in his room and turn off the power, but I don't know what else to do."

Suzanne had tears in her eyes when she finished her tirade. I took her in my arms. She put her head on my shoulder. Would it be completely inappropriate to kiss her?

"I'm sorry. It's exhausting sometimes," she said.

"I was a little quirky at that age too, and I turned out all right. Okay, that's not cheering you up. We'll figure it out. I promise. I know I haven't been around enough, but I am not going to leave you alone with this."

This time she kissed me. It was a quick peck, but I could still taste it on my slow run home. I didn't want to worry her, but she was right, Devon was up to something. It couldn't be too bad. He never left his room and his grades were holding up, but he obviously felt guilty about it.

I felt bad about bugging my own son, but Devon was smart enough to stonewall me unless I had the goods. The best interrogations are when you knew what you're looking for, when the information asymmetry is on your side. It gave me an idea about Westfield. He knew more than we did. That had to change.

· · · · · · · · · ·

I described what I had in mind to Pratt and Caroline. Pratt didn't pick his head up from his computer. Caroline sat behind him, looking over his shoulder.

"We're safe here. If we buy time, Danny can crack their encryption and give us a better idea of who we're dealing with," Caroline said.

"You're talking about safety? I'm going to have to change your nickname," I said.

"It's too late. I already had the Angel of Death t-shirts made."

"Good. Because you can bet they have every resource they can put their hands on looking for us. And when they find us, we won't be safe and neither will my family. I'm not going to wait around for that."

"Tell me what I need to do," Pratt said.

Caroline gave him a look like a mom who was disappointed that her kid wasn't listening to her.

I gave Pratt the details, and while he worked I banged out another chapter for Connor, "How to Cut the Jugular Vein," to pass the time.

"Wouldn't it be simpler to use a gun?" Caroline asked.

"Since the book is called *Stabbing Weapons for Morons*, that would sort of defeat the purpose."

"That's a stupid name for a book."

"Which is perfect, because only stupid people will buy it," I said.

"You risk your life for your country and plumbers get paid more."

"They have better unions."

"Maybe we should start one. We could all go on strike unless they pay us more."

"That could work. Or they'd kill us," I said.

"Do you ever wonder whether it's worth it?"

"Not when I get to meet interesting people like you."

"I mean it. Do you ever think about disappearing, starting over with a real life," she said.

"I can't be a plumber, I'm no good with my hands."

She didn't laugh.

"Yes, I think about it every day. But I have an ex-wife and a son. What am I supposed to do, confess everything and tell them we have to disappear now? How could I ask them to give up everything and everyone they know? I've been thinking about it a lot lately. There's only one way this job ends. And it's not with a retirement party."

She nodded slowly. It felt good to know she understood. It's not something I could share with anyone else, not even Rob. I couldn't risk his deciding I was unreliable. He wouldn't want to have me retired, but I had no doubt he would do what he had to.

"Are you hungry? I'm hungry. I'm going to get some burgers at Burger and Brew," I said.

She smiled at me. It wasn't one of her dazzling, "I'm going to put you under my spell smiles." It felt real.

I called in the order but it wasn't ready when I got there. I sipped a ginger ale while I waited. I don't drink during an operation. The place was filling up with suburban dads on the way home from the train station looking for a quick drink before facing domestic bliss. A couple of guys at the end of the bar were rifling beers and laughing like frat boys. One of them was a short fat guy and the other was Rowan. I edged closer to listen.

"I'm telling you, I throw the ball at his head and the little spaz still can't figure it out. I keep yelling, 'use your head' at him," Rowan said and high-fived his friend.

"Fighting angry is fighting to lose," Nachash said in my head.

"Fuck that," was my response.

Rowan and his buddy were at the end of the bar near the bathroom. It wasn't hard to get behind Rowan. Then I waited until a tall, barrel-chested, local fireman came out the bathroom. I timed it so he was moving past me. I hit Rowan with an elbow to the kidney. It wasn't enough to make him piss blood, but it hurt plenty. With the other hand, I grabbed the back of the fireman's shirt and yanked him back toward Rowan, and then spun out of the way and into the bathroom.

I cracked the door and watched. Rowan turned around. The fireman tumbled into him. Rowan thought the fireman was a drunk who had hit him. The fireman thought Rowan had grabbed him.

"What the fuck is wrong with you?" Rowan demanded.

"Are you trying to be funny?" The local blue-collar guys don't like to take shit from the yuppie-come-latelies in town.

"You hit me," Rowan said. He looked sideways at his buddy who subtly edged away.

"If you can't hold your beer like a big boy, then Mommy shouldn't let you out."

I enjoyed the look of fear in Rowan's eyes. I could see him searching for something to say that didn't feel like total capitulation.

"I'm a doctor. I know how much to drink."

For a moment I thought that the fireman was going to slug him. It was a nice moment. Then he laughed in Rowan's face. "All right, Doc, you get home safely now." They don't make firemen like they used to. He laughed again and bellied up to the bar.

Rowan turned to his buddy and whispered. The buddy nodded with one eye on the fireman to make sure he couldn't hear. Rowan was clearly rationalizing at full speed. He wasn't scared. The fireman wasn't worth his time. That's why the town needed to gentrify more. I replayed the scene in my mind a few times on the walk home. It wasn't as much fun as if the fireman had hit him, but I enjoyed it as much as I could.

Pratt worked right through dinner. I tried to get some writing done, but Caroline turned off my computer and led me into the bedroom.

"I'm starting to feel like you only love me for my body," I said.

"Sorry to disappoint you, but I wanted to talk where Danny couldn't hear us."

"So you only want me for my mind?"

"It depends on how the talk goes," she said.

"In that case, I'm here to listen."

"I'm worried about him. He's going to burn himself out."

"Slow him down. You two don't seem to have problems communicating," I said.

"He looks up to you. From me, it sounds like I'm trying to mother him."

"Oh, is that what you're doing."

"I'm not sleeping with Danny if that's what you're implying. I like that you're jealous though."

"Time isn't on our side. He can handle this a little longer," I said.

"He thinks you're going to take care of him. He trusts you."

"I don't know how this is going to end up for Pratt. I don't know how it's going to end up for you and me. I'm trying to get us through tomorrow."

"One day at a time. One hour at a time. One minute at a time. That's how they train you, right?" she said.

"The only way to stay sane."

"In an insane world."

"Until you stop knowing whether you're a suburban dad who is secretly a contractor or a contractor who is posing as a suburban dad," I said.

"Dr. Jekyll and Mr. *Hide*. No one gets to know the real you. Even you. Well, I think you do know who you are, no matter how much you fight it."

"Yeah, who am I?" I said.

"One of the good guys," she said, kissed me on the lips and walked out the door.

"What about wanting me for my body?"

"You satisfied me fully with your mind," she said.

She went back to keep an eye on Pratt. I figured, if I wasn't going to be kept busy, I might as well get some sleep. We had a big day ahead of us. I had barely dozed off when I heard a piercing scream. Mimi had made another sneak attack, but this time, she was the one who was screaming. When I reached the bathroom, I found out why. Mimi was standing face to face with a dripping wet, totally naked Caroline.

"Mimi meet Caroline. Caroline this is Mimi."

Mimi slapped me across the face and left. I could have blocked it, but I thought it might make her feel better.

"Your girlfriend didn't seem happy to meet me," Caroline said.

"She's just my neighbor." It didn't sound fair when I said it, not fair to Mimi. Was it her ego that was hurt, or did she have real feelings for me? It had never occurred to me. It probably should have.

"We can play neighbor too," Caroline said and undressed me.

I almost asked her where Pratt was, as if we were sneaking a quickie while our toddler took a nap. She sat me on the toilet seat and mounted me, and all thoughts of Pratt were gone. It takes strong legs to manage seated sex. I put one hand on each calf to feel her muscles work. They were developed enough to form a tight curve, but not bulgy or overbuilt. It's funny what turns you on when you get older. She gracefully angled herself forward, sliding against me with every thrust. Still wet from the shower, she formed the perfect suction. It was like she sensed that my time away from her might have broken her spell and now she cast it all over again. She did everything but walk me back to bed and tuck me in.

CHAPTER NINE

W e mobilized in the morning like we were a team. We made good time into the City. No one was following us.

Caroline and Pratt quietly set up on the roof of the apartment across the street from Pratt's building. I walked through the front door and took my time. I climbed the stairs to his apartment, elevators can quickly turn into death traps, and noisily let myself in. I opened all the windows.

I assumed that all three of the groups that were chasing Tiresias would have some kind of surveillance set up. Whoever showed up first got to be interrogated. It was up to Caroline to make sure that the other groups didn't crash the party. I had considered moving the interrogation to another location, but if the other groups showed up while we were on the move, it would leave us vulnerable.

"Three white males entering the building. Pratt says they aren't residents," Caroline said in my wireless earpiece.

When they broke down the door and charged in, guns drawn, they were surprised to find me sitting calmly on the living room couch waiting for them. Since they were carrying Commanders, I assumed they were Russian.

"*Gavno, mudak, blyat,*" was my phonetically pronounced greeting. That roughly translated to "shit, asshole, whore." They were the three curses I knew in Russian.

"Where's the computer genius?" the middle of the three asked in unaccented English.

"If I had known you spoke this well, I would have cursed you out in English," I said.

"It won't be so funny when . . ."

My new Russian friend stopped in midsentence as his two comrades turned to jelly. A bullet from my sniper rifle, in Caroline's capable hands, had noiselessly passed through the open windows and taken them in the head.

"You might want to put your gun down," I said.

He lowered it slowly to the floor.

"Please, take a seat." I stood up and motioned him to take my place on the couch. "We haven't formally met yet. What's your name?"

He closed his eyes. I registered my unhappiness with his bad manners by spraying him in the face with a small fire extinguisher I had brought with me. I don't believe in waterboarding. Some interrogators like it because it always gets a confession. When you feel like you're drowning, you will confess to anything. The problem is that you can't rely on the information. They will spit out anything they can come up with to make you stop. Over time, you might get enough out of the interrogation to piece things together, but it's not efficient. Creating enough discomfort for motivation but not enough that you taint the information is an art, but we were in a hurry, I used what I had.

"I'm sorry. That must have been unpleasant. Now tell me your name so I don't have to do it again."

"Go fuck yourself," was his answer.

"Good. Now we're talking. Tell me who sent you and I'll let you go. I'm not interested in hostages."

He shook his head. We were going backward. I stuck the fire extinguisher nozzle in his mouth and sprayed, enough to show him I meant business. Some interrogators enjoy doing their business. Not all of them are sadists. Some enjoy the control. Some like the psychological battle. I don't take pleasure in any of it. Nachash said I needed to suppress my empathy. I was less concerned about controlling my empathy than losing it. You run across some cold-blooded characters in this business. It's like they stop being human. You can't turn that on and off.

"Don't make me do that again. It's not worth it. I know who sent you. You know I know. All I need is for you to confirm it. Then I can tell my boss I got something out of you and I can call it a day. We don't have much time here."

He shook his head, but not as emphatically. His resolve was breaking. If I had more time, I could have worked him verbally. I stuck the nozzle back in his mouth and gave him a long pull. He vomited white foam onto the floor. His skin turned gray. His eyes watered. He spat out bile and tried to clear his head.

"The next one will probably drown you. That would be a shame. Just tell me who sent you."

Once he told me something, it wouldn't be hard to get every-thing. It's that first leap that's hardest. I could feel his conflict. He was convincing himself that it was okay to tell me. It was a matter of time.

"Six white males entering the building," Caroline said in my earpiece.

"Six? What's wrong with them? Do they think I have a small battalion in here?" That was too many to control.

"Get up," I said to the Russian. "We're moving."

He didn't respond. Events were moving too quickly for him. I took his arm and pulled him to his feet. He stumbled and lurched against me as a bullet took him below the right shoulder blade. If he hadn't tripped, it would have been his head.

"Cease fire. Repeat, cease fire," I screamed at Caroline.

The Russian was too heavy to drag. "Sorry, that wasn't supposed to happen," I said, easing him back down onto the couch.

I ran to Pratt's room and descended the fire escape. I met Caroline and Pratt at my car, which I had parked a few blocks away.

"I thought he was attacking you," Caroline said, once we were safely away.

Was she lying? I couldn't tell. And I wasn't sure how much my feelings were getting in the way of my reason. It's amazing how we can project all sorts of ridiculous fantasies on attractive women. I'm sure Nachash would have something annoying to say about it.

"Where are we going?" Pratt asked, as I slowly drove uptown.

"I don't know yet," I answered, pulling out my phone and opening my tracker app. "I put a dot on the Russian. Let's see where his new friends take him."

It didn't take long for the six yahoos to grab the Russian and throw him in their van. We tracked them to an abandoned pet store in Hunts Point. It said, "Vinny's Pets" across a big front window. The glass was cracked and I didn't see any pets. It used to be that you could find safe houses on the western and northern fringes of Manhattan, but now they were full of family buildings and Starbucks. Even Brooklyn was too gentrified and Queens was on the way. The Bronx was the last bastion of burned out buildings and deserted shops. Hunts Point was on the water. There were a lot of import-export companies there, but the crime rate was high, so outside of business hours there weren't a lot of nosy neighbors.

We parked around the corner, did a quick scout, and didn't see any lookouts. The front door was nailed shut from the outside with planks of wood running across. It wasn't the type of building that would have roof access, but there would likely be a bathroom in the back. I wedged myself sideways down a narrow alley that ran along the side of the store. Bathrooms typically have windows that face out. This one didn't have much of a view, looking right at the building across the alley, but it was big enough for me to wriggle through. It was secured by a rusted-out metal screen. I was up-to-date on my tetanus shot. I got a firm grip and pulled.

It came away easily in my hands. I pried open the window and pulled myself through. The smell was overpowering. My guess was that it hadn't been kept very clean when Vinny was still selling pets. Now it was a full-fledged health hazard. I felt a vibration in my pocket and for a moment I thought it was the room's bacteria climbing into my clothes. I pulled out my phone. It was Suzanne calling. If it was an emergency, she would call back, and there was nothing I could do now anyway. I needed to take care of the business at hand.

I cracked the bathroom door and got a side view of a back-room where the Russian was locked in a dog cage. The Suit was literally rattling his cage, running the butt of his gun across the bars. This wasn't what I expected. The Israelis were unlikely to have sent five agents to reinforce him, so Caroline had lied.

The safest play would be to hit him, grab the Russian, and interrogate him before he bled out. I could try to subdue the Suit, but getting the drop on someone is harder than it sounds, a lot of things can go wrong. Like he can turn and shoot, which would be stupid because you would probably kill him, but he might kill you too, and who's laughing then? But having two subjects to interrogate is a huge advantage. You can match their stories and play them against each other. And the disgusting bathroom was sending my germophobia into overdrive. At least I could shoot the Suit. I had no defense against the germs.

"I'm sorry about your partner," I said, as I stepped out of the bathroom. "Put your gun down unless you want to join him."

The Suit turned very calmly like he'd been expecting me. He didn't raise his gun, but he didn't put it down either.

"Don't make me count to three, it makes me feel stupid," I said.

"Fuck you," was the Suit's response.

"I'm not going to take offense, because I understand you're a little pissed, but this is your last chance to drop your gun before I shoot you in your potty mouth."

I don't know whether he was going to put it down or not. I didn't get the chance to find out, because the lights went out. I fired. I heard a yell of pain. I fired again.

The lights came back on and I saw that the Suit had pivoted sideways and my shots had hit the Russian in the cage behind him. The Russian looked dead. The Suit was very much alive and had his massive Desert Eagle pointed at me. Luckily, the lights blinded him and his shot went wide.

He fired again as I swiveled in his direction to return fire, but Caroline messed up my shot. She had entered the room while it was dark and she dove into me at full speed. My shot went high. Caroline took the Suit's bullet.

She landed hard, her head bouncing off the floor. Her momentum knocked me down too. By the time I popped up, the Suit had fled out the back door. I didn't have to check to make sure the Russian was dead. The cage was pooled with blood. Caroline was doing her share of bleeding too.

Pratt ran into the room, saw all the blood and started retching.

"Where are you hit?" I asked Caroline.

She pointed to her shoulder. She was groggy, probably had a concussion.

"We'll get you out on the street and call 911. Tell them it was a mugging gone wrong. In this neighborhood they'll believe it."

"No hospital. Westfield will be watching them. You take care of it." The concussion had her slurring her words.

"I'm not a doctor."

"I'm not a patient. Do a field dressing and take me home."

"It's filthy in here. You could get infected."

"Do it!"

She was impossible to argue with. It reminded me of Suzanne. The bullet had sliced through the top of her left shoulder, no arteries had been hit. She would survive if I didn't screw it up too badly.

"Take off your shirt," I said to Pratt.

He managed to stop gagging long enough to unbutton it and hand it to me.

"Give me a cuff link," I added.

I pressed the side of the cuff link and the blade popped out. I used it to cut his shirt into strips and then wrapped the wound with them. The idea was to keep enough pressure on it to control the bleeding but not enough that it cut off her circulation.

"Don't be a pussy. You can make it tighter than that." She growled something that sounded like "*Tchaaaa*" to punctuate her point.

I'd never heard that one. She probably knew how to curse in more languages than I did. I peered into Caroline's eyes. She was responsive and could follow my finger when I moved it in front of her. She definitely had a concussion and probably mild shock, but I didn't see signs of a brain bleed. I dressed the wound, which slowed the bleeding, but we still had to get her out of there. If I were the Suit, I would either stake out a building tall enough that I had a shot at us whether we came out the front or the back, or the roof of the pet shop. I peered out the back and then the front door. Riflescopes can catch the light if you're not careful. I didn't see anything, but that didn't mean much. The Suit was a pro. I scooped Caroline up and carried her to the front of the store.

"I can walk," she protested.

"I just got you bandaged. I'm not going to let you start bleeding all over the place again."

"You have a terrible bedside manner," she said.

I put her down by the front door and took off my vest.

"If our friend is out there, he wants you alive," I said to Pratt. "You're going to put her in a fireman's carry. I'm going to drape my vest over her. And you're going to carry her to the car. It's only a few feet. Can you do that?"

"I'm stronger than I look," he said.

"Let's hope so. The vest won't leave him much of a target. Anything exposed should be too close to your head for him to get a comfortable shot, but you still want to move quickly."

"I don't like this plan," he said.

"I'll cover you. If he gives his position away I'll hit him. Make sure she keeps her head down once she's in the car."

"How do you get to the car?" he asked.

"Get it moving as soon as you're in. Leave the door open. I'll follow."

"This is a bad plan," he said.

I picked Caroline up in a fireman's carry to show Pratt what he needed to do. "You're going to carry her like this. Pretend she's a sack of flour. Keep your back straight and flex your knees slightly, take the weight in your legs."

"I like flowers. Why don't you buy me flowers?" Caroline said. Suzanne used to ask me the same thing.

Pratt bent his knees and straightened his back trying to mimic what I had shown him. He looked like a constipated duck. I laid Caroline across his shoulders and draped my vest over her. Pratt's legs shook, but he didn't drop her.

"Don't stop no matter what happens," I said.

I unlocked the car with my key fob and pressed the keys into Pratt's hand. I shouldered his backpack and gave him a gentle shove out the door. I crouched in the doorway, presenting as small a target as possible. I had my Browning clasped with two hands in front of me. I scanned the rooftops and the car-line ready to react. Assuming the Suit had a rifle, he would likely set up out of my range, but I would give the best cover I could.

Pratt dumped Caroline in the front passenger seat, climbed over her, and got the car started in good time. No shots were fired. I stayed low and dived into the car on top of Caroline. Pratt pulled out and sideswiped the car in front of us. He didn't seem to notice.

He screamed down the street, pushing the pedal to the floor. I wanted to tell him to turn onto a side street, but I was afraid he'd roll the car. I kept my eye on the side view mirror and didn't pick up anyone following.

"Pull over, Hot Rod," I said.

Pratt hit the brake too hard and sent me banging into the dashboard. He yanked the wheel and brought us nose first to the curb.

"I like driving. I'm getting better at it," he said.

I took the wheel and exiled him to the back seat. "What happened with the lights? Was that you?" I asked him.

"He had reinforcements coming."

"You saw them?"

"Caroline did."

"And she told you to hit the lights?"

"I had to warn you."

"Sending a text would warn me. Bird sounds would warn me. Smoke signals would warn me. Hitting the lights almost killed me. You only want to hit the lights if I'm in an inferior position. Then it can balance the odds. What you did was get one of our interrogation subjects killed and let the other get away." I didn't exactly yell, but I was frustrated. The look on Pratt's face was like when I used to lose my temper with Devon when he was a toddler. I knew I was being a bad parent, but I couldn't stop. The adrenaline was starting to wear off and my nerves were vibrating. I could hear Nachash whisper his disappointment.

"You think Caroline made it up about the other agents?" Pratt said. "She saved your life. It doesn't make sense."

Not much made sense. The disappearing and reappearing agents, Caroline taking a bullet for me, the Suit running off, none of it fit. The Suit should have tried to pick us off when we went for the car. He had us in a vulnerable position. I wouldn't have passed that up.

We made good time back to my house. Suzanne was seated on the front steps, and she didn't look pleased. I had forgotten to call her back. I pulled into the garage, told Pratt to get Caroline into the house and ran to head off Suzanne before she followed us.

"Is everything okay?" I was pretty sure she wouldn't be sitting there if Devon was hurt, but Suzanne had never shown up at my house unannounced.

"Maybe we should ask the young blonde woman who was in your car?"

"She's one of Connor's writers. He wants us to work together on a new book—*Hot Chicks for Morons*. The kid is our research assistant."

"I'm not one of your moron readers," she said.

"You're probably the smartest person I know, and this is only work."

"Okay, then let's go inside and you can introduce me to your coworker."

"She's not feeling well. The kid took her inside to lie down."

The look on Suzanne's face broke my heart.

"I should have known better. Why would all the secrets and half-truths stop now?" she said.

"Suzanne, I promise you, this isn't . . ."

"Don't," she practically spat. "Don't promise me anything. Don't make up excuses to see me. Don't pretend you've changed. I can deal with you being a selfish liar. I can't deal with you pretending that you're not."

She stormed away, and I couldn't go after her. I had to tend to Caroline. And I wasn't sure what I could say to Suzanne anyway. I gave myself exactly sixty seconds to feel sorry for myself and then put those feelings away. I used a self-hypnosis trick Nachash had taught me. Suzanne had left Gib, and I felt bad for him, but there was nothing I could do to help. It was like I had two screens in my head. I put Gib on the left screen and turned my focus to the right one. On the right one, all that mattered was helping Caroline. Gib didn't exist. It was like icy water on burned skin. It wouldn't heal the wound, but it cooled the pain, for now.

Caroline was laid out on my couch. The bleeding had started again, staining the couch cushions and the rug. This job was getting way too expensive. If I survived, I was going to have to beg Connor for more work.

I washed my hands carefully and took out my medical kit. I donned surgical gloves and spread a square of sterile latex on the coffee table next to the couch. I placed on it a syringe, a bottle of saline solution, a bottle of benzoin, a tube of lidocaine ointment, sterile swabs, surgical scissors, and a suture needle with absorbable suture material attached.

I filled the syringe with saline solution and irrigated the wound. There weren't any foreign bodies. The bullet had made a clean crease in the shoulder. I swabbed lidocaine on the area to numb it.

"You doing okay?" I said.

"Yup," Pratt and Caroline answered in unison.

Pratt looked like he was going to start gagging again.

"Why don't you go work on cracking that encryption," I said.

He took the hint and beat a hasty retreat.

"This is going to hurt a little," I told Caroline.

"Get it done. We have work to do."

The shock was wearing off, which was a good sign. I used mattress stitches about two millimeters apart to close Caroline's wound. The work would never be mistaken for plastic surgery, but I felt an odd satisfaction when it was done. It was nice to use my hands to help someone for a change.

"Thanks, Doc," she said sitting up.

"You need to rest. Doctor's orders."

She tried to stand and failed. "Maybe I'll rest a little. Tell me a story. My father always told me a story when he put me to bed," she said, lying back down.

"I'm terrible with bedtime stories. Devon used to kick me out and demand that Suzanne take over."

"My ex was a terrible storyteller too."

"Is that why you broke up? Because Suzanne had a much longer list of grievances."

"He always had to be right. The world was black and white, and only he knew which was which."

"Why did you marry him?"

"Comforting for a while. I always knew he wanted me. Never had to get jealous." She was too sleepy for complete sentences. "Then all I wanted to do was prove him wrong."

"About what?"

"Everything."

"That must have been fun," I said.

"But I did it."

"Did what?" I said.

"Proved him wrong. He thought we would always be together."

I sat in the armchair and gently roused her every fifteen minutes to make sure there was no cranial bleeding, that was the protocol. With everything that was out of control, it felt good that I could keep her safe.

CHAPTER TEN

"Have you found anything on Westfield yet?"

From counting the Starburst wrappers, it looked like Pratt had been up all night working on his computer.

"You can't rush these things," Pratt responded.

I tried to clean the stains out of the carpet with mixed success. It no longer looked like blood, but the color of the carpet had turned to a disturbing orange. The couch was a lost cause. I would have to drape a blanket over it until I had time to replace it.

I hadn't gotten much rest myself, watching over Caroline. I'm not sure I would have slept anyway. I had peeked in on Suzanne using the Big House's webcams. I felt bad about violating her privacy, but I couldn't help myself. Watching her cry and Rowan comfort her was my punishment. I clicked off before it went beyond that, but I couldn't get the image out of my mind.

They were all out of the house now. It was time for a visit. "Keep an eye on Caroline. You need to check her every half hour," I said.

Pratt nodded and was back to work. I was beginning to lose hope that he was ever going to crack the CIA servers, and the clock was ticking. Westfield would uncover my identity and where I lived eventually. I had to figure out a way to unravel what was going on and get to him first.

I took a jog to the Big House. I came at it from the rear and let myself in the back door. I didn't want a nosy neighbor telling Suzanne I'd dropped by.

The webcam I had planted in Devon's room had captured him inputting his password. I had watched the feed from the camera as Devon sat alone at his computer. His face had been completely intent. It reminded me too much of Pratt.

I plugged a thumb drive into his computer and downloaded every file and folder on the hard drive. I uploaded an industrial strength decryption program and worked my way through a few that were encrypted. I also uploaded a spyware program that would let me follow what he was doing on his computer remotely. I could have had Pratt hack into his computer for me, but that seemed like a bigger violation of Devon's privacy. This was between the two of us. I sneaked back out, dropped my child support check in the mailbox and jogged home.

I looked at the encrypted files first. It was a fairly typical collection of porn and fantasy game stuff. It looked like he and his friends had been pranking some of their classmates, sending porn to them anonymously. Visualizing those uptight private school kids seeing porn pop up made me smile. I couldn't figure out exactly what the fantasy stuff was about, but it looked like they were hacking into gaming sites to steal virtual weapons and such. Not a great hobby, but a victimless crime. I waited for Devon to come home and followed what he did on his computer to make sure there wasn't anything else going on.

He connected to at least three other IP addresses, presumably his partners in crime. They used a sophisticated proxy set up to disguise themselves. Where did they learn all of this? Maybe I should enlist them to help Pratt. I expected to see a parade of fantasy game images. Instead, I saw names, numbers, and letters. As the numbers changed, I realized what I was seeing. Now I knew why he was getting such good grades without doing his homework. They were hacking into the school's server to change their grades.

I would have to confront Devon without letting Suzanne know. If she found out, she would freak out for real. Of course, if she got wind of it and realized I didn't tell her, she'd never forgive me. Not that I was sure she would forgive me as it was. There was only one bright side. I figured out what Rob was trying to tell me when he showed up at Devon's school. He knew what Devon was up to, and he wanted to make sure I knew.

Pratt was at his computer. Caroline had dozed off on the couch.

"We need to talk," I whispered to Pratt.

"About what?" he asked.

I hand signaled him to lower his voice. "When you yelled at Westfield, you said, 'We know who you are. We know who the dirty one is.'"

"You, Caroline, and me."

"That's what I thought at the time. But that's not what you meant, was it? It's you and your coworkers. You're not trying to find Westfield. You're still working on Tiresias. That's why you wanted to go back to Advanced Crypto. There was code on their servers that you hadn't been able to get out. You and a bunch of your buddies are working together to finish the program and sell it to the highest bidder."

"We would never do that."

"My contact went a long way to warn me that you were collaborating with others on this. It's the only thing that makes sense."

"Of course. He knew exactly what we were doing. But we would never sell the code. We are going to make it open source."

"You mean like anyone can use it?" I said.

"Including hackers all over the world. It won't take them long to figure out a way to protect against it."

"If that's true, why not upload it right now," I said.

"If a foreign government, or a terrorist group, or our government for that matter, managed to finish it first, they would be able to use it until everyone else caught up. We can't take that chance."

If it was a lie, it was a good one. No matter who had the program, you always had to worry that it would fall into the wrong hands. This was the only way to permanently neutralize it.

"Why the whistleblower complaint? That gave you away."

"They were onto me already. The complaint was a red herring," he said.

"You still would have ended up renditioned if Rob hadn't alerted me."

"But he did, so it all worked out."

It was a well-thought-out plan. It was too well-thought-out for a civilian. "Rob tipped you, didn't he? You thought I was there to save you at Starbucks because Rob told you I would."

"Then you acted like you had no idea what was going on," Pratt said.

"I didn't. Rob liked to play mind games. He probably figured I would fight him if he told me he wanted to go against the Agency like this. He set me up where he knew I'd save you."

"That was smart," Pratt said.

"He completely manipulated both of us and that's your reaction?"

"He was right. You saved my life."

"But you still couldn't trust me with the truth?" I said.

"He told me that you would figure it out when the time was right."

"And why did you trust him?" I asked.

"The same reason you did. He recruited me."

And that was the rest of Rob's message. In the spy world, Pratt was Rob's progeny, and he had gotten mixed up in something that was over his head, like Devon had. Rob thought I would figure out the message, because I would pick up on what Devon was doing. If I were a better father, I would have.

"You were the one at Advanced Crypto who was supposed to keep an eye out for coders who might pose a security risk. Except you were also the one who ended up going rogue," I said.

"To be fair, I created most of the code. It only seems right that I should have a say in what's done with it."

"I'm pretty sure they don't see it that way."

"That's why I had no choice. I signed up to help get the bad guys, not to be one of them. Rob said you were the same way," he said.

It touched me that this was how Pratt saw me, as a wide-eyed idealist like him. Had I ever been that innocent?

"Did he give you the disappointed older brother act when he found out what you were up to?"

"More like disappointed dad," he said without trying to be mean. "He told me that he would fix it if I shut down what we were doing. I told him I couldn't do that. He got very quiet, shook his head. It made me feel really bad."

"That's the point," I said.

"He said to give him time to figure out what to do, but Westfield must have found out what we were doing first."

"He told you that?" I asked.

Pratt shook his head. "Rob showed up at my apartment in the middle of the night. He said I was in danger but it was going to be okay, he had a guy whom he trusted. He said he would make sure I didn't get hurt."

"He left you there as bait. He didn't know for sure who he was dealing with, so he waited to see who moved on you," I said.

Rob's level of manipulation was stunning. It was beyond anything I could have dreamed up. Manipulation was an unavoidable part of the job, but it shouldn't be the whole job.

"The Russians, the Israelis, and Westfield and his crazy group of contractors are all after us, and Rob hasn't left us a clue how they found out about you or what their plans are."

"They all want Tiresias, and I'm not going to let them have it," Pratt said proudly.

I laughed despite myself.

"What?" he said.

"I wish it were that easy. We need to find out what each group knows and what their plans are, if we're going to have any chance of surviving this. And we need to find Westfield. He's the key. We need to find him before he finds us. The moral high ground feels a lot better when you're not buried in it."

"I'm not a martyr. I don't want to die. I just want to do the right thing," he said.

"Hard to argue with that," Caroline said.

I wondered how long she had been awake and listening. "Just learning some new things about our boy," I said.

"He's full of surprises," she said.

She knew what Pratt had been up to. What was her agenda? Did she shoot the Russian because she thought he was moving on me, or was she trying to make sure I didn't find out too much? And what about the five phantom Israelis that she claimed were with the Suit? A straight-ahead interrogation was unlikely to work with her, and I might lose Pratt in the process. Keeping her close and waiting for the right time to crack her story was my best bet.

"Caroline and I are going for a ride. You know what I need you to do."

"Are we going to a drive-in or do you have somewhere else you like to make out?" Caroline asked me.

"Not unless you're turned on by doctor's offices."

"I told you, I won't go to a hospital."

"I'm not taking you to one."

"Doctor's offices are almost as risky. As soon as they file the paperwork, we are at risk."

"There won't be any paperwork," I said.

. . . .

I hadn't been to the office in years. Caroline seemed fine from her concussion, but if she dropped dead from a brain bleed, I'd feel really bad about it. Everything looked the same in the waiting room. Mrs. Levine, the receptionist, looked like she was about a hundred years old, but she had always looked ancient to me.

"We need ten minutes with him," I said.

"Do you have an appointment?" she asked, though she knew we didn't.

"Please tell him I'm here. We won't take long."

Mrs. Levine reluctantly picked up the phone and engaged the old-fashioned intercom system. She cupped her hand and whispered into the receiver. After some back and forth where I'm sure she advocated for sending us on our way, she waved us back.

"Treatment room one. You know the way," she said.

Caroline looked at me quizzically but didn't ask any questions. The treatment room was immaculate. The nurses bustling around were almost as old as Mrs. Levine and as practiced at their craft. The office was staffed entirely by women. There was only one rooster in the coop and that was the doctor.

"You're always welcome here, Gibbons, but you could have called. Mrs. Levine doesn't like surprises," the doctor said.

"Mrs. Levine would have told me that you didn't have any openings until next century," I said.

"That's why I've kept her all these years."

From anyone else I would have suspected this was meant to be funny.

"Well you're here. What can I do for you? And who is this young lady?" the doctor said.

"Caroline had a bullet wound in her right shoulder stitched up and suffered a concussion. She needs to be looked at off the books. No insurance, no records."

"My name is Doctor Alexander," he said to Caroline. "Are you in some kind of trouble?"

"Alexander? Are you . . . ?"

"Caroline, meet my father. He's going to examine you and spare you all the annoying questions that he would like to ask."

"Nice to meet you. I was in the wrong place at the wrong time. It would be embarrassing for my family if that were to be made public. Your son was kind enough to offer your help. If you're not comfortable with that, we will leave with no hard feelings," Caroline said.

"My son knows that I would never turn away a patient. Gibbons, you may leave the room and let me conduct my examination."

"I'll see you outside, *Gibbons*," Caroline said.

My father actually smiled at her. If she could charm *him*, Pratt and I had no chance. The waiting room was crowded as usual. Mrs. Levine orchestrated patients filling out forms, handing over insurance cards, and submitting copays. She still found time to give me a few of her trademark glares. She had never liked it when my father brought me to the office and she still didn't. Finally, she gestured me back in without a word.

"Time has done nothing to improve your dexterity," was my father's greeting.

"But no sign of infection, right?"

"That much you managed. I see no sign of a brain bleed either, but she was clearly concussed. She should avoid rigorous activity for at least a week."

"Whatever you say, Dr. A," Caroline said.

Anyone else calling my father Dr. A would have gotten a look of death. My father gave her a paternal smile I didn't know he possessed. The truth was that I had a doctor in Yonkers who took care of me when I needed absolute discretion. I could have taken Caroline to him. My father was a better doctor, of course, and I wanted to see Caroline work her magic on him. Maybe I wanted him to believe I was romantically involved with her. He had come to like Suzanne and saw our divorce as my failure.

"Your dad's an interesting character," Caroline commented when we were back in the Camry.

"That was his best behavior."

"He must be great in the operating room. He gives you that feeling like he's totally in control. He knows exactly what to do, but he doesn't need to shove it in your face to prove it. Kind of like you," she said.

"Look, we both know you're playing me. That's part of the game, and I can't say I'm not enjoying it. But you don't need to pretend it's real," I said.

"Why are you sure it isn't? How many girls would take a bullet for you?"

"And I didn't get you flowers. How about you tell me what you're after? I'll do everything I can to make sure you get it," I said.

"I believe you would if you could. But I don't want you to make promises you can't keep. You're not that kind of guy."

My phone buzzed before I could say anything else. It was Suzanne.

"I'm glad you called. I need you to know that there is nothing going on with Caroline."

Caroline blew in my ear.

"I didn't call to hear more of your lies. Your check bounced. Drop over another one when I'm not there. And add twenty bucks for the fee the bank charged me," she said.

"There's plenty of money in that account."

Caroline licked my ear lobe.

"This is irresponsible even for you. You're not just hurting me, this affects Devon too," Suzanne said.

"I promise you that I will figure out what's going on and fix it."

"Don't promise. Do it," Suzanne said.

Suzanne hung up. Caroline bit my ear.

"Why is she being such a bitch?" Caroline said.

"She's got a lot going on. And I don't always make it easy."

"You are still in love with her."

"She's my wife."

"Ex-wife."

"Once a wife, always a wife."

"Not for me. My cliché of choice is, 'done is done.' Or we could go with 'once an asshole, always an asshole,'" Caroline said.

"I thought *you* dumped *him*. I mean I get he was a difficult guy, but what did he do to hurt you so badly?'

"Nothing worse than a bullet to the shoulder. And at least he didn't pretend nothing was going on," Caroline said.

"It's not like I can tell her the truth."

"Make sure to tell yourself the truth," Caroline said.

I wanted to question her more, but she slid down in her seat and went to sleep, or pretended to. She bounded out of the car when we got home and got to the house before me. She stood in the door and laughed. I followed her and saw why. Pratt was sitting on the couch flanked by two Pratt-a-likes. They were the same age, dressed in the same brightly colored jeans and cuff-linked shirts, and banging away on their laptops in unison.

"This is Ben and Todd. I told them they would be safe here," was Pratt's explanation.

"Then you lied. The second they knew where I lived they became a risk to my family. If Westfield doesn't take care of them, now I'll have to."

"I picked them up in an Uber. I blindfolded them and masked your router. They have no idea where they are or who you are. They won't take any images of you, and they'll never hear your name. I'm not stupid, you know."

"You took a *stupid* risk. What if one of Westfield's contractors followed them here?" I said.

Pratt would probably be gone, and I would have been greeted by a bullet to the head if they had been followed, but I couldn't let him off that easily.

"Danny made sure we were clean," Ben said.

"He's good at that kind of thing," Todd added.

I was about to ask him why he thought he was qualified to judge that when Devon walked into the living room carrying a plate of burritos.

"Are those the vegetarian ones?" Pratt asked.

"We're out of those," I answered before Devon could. "Does your mom know you're here?" I asked Devon.

"I told her I was staying after school at the computer lab. I might be in trouble," he said, doling out the burritos to Todd and Ben.

"We used to be vegetarians," Todd said.

"But we like meat too much," Ben added.

Pratt shook his head. Caroline took his burrito.

"Why don't we go into my bedroom," I said to Devon. "These guys are helping me with my research for my next Moron book, and we're behind."

"They told me."

Pratt gave me a self-satisfied smile. I wanted to strangle him.

Devon and I sat on my bed in my room.

"Those guys are totally cool. Can I get an old-fashioned shirt like they wear?" Devon said.

It was a horrifying thought, but at least Pratt didn't hear him say it. "We can talk about your wardrobe later. What's going on?"

"I got called into the headmaster's office. He thinks a couple of friends and me have been hacking into the school server and changing grades."

"Why would he think that?"

I hoped he wouldn't lie to me. I didn't want to interrogate him. I wanted to lie in bed and hear about the diorama he made about the first moon flight.

"We were careful. I still don't know how we got caught. Tyler says someone must have been spoofing us and tripped the security protocol, but he's always paranoid," Devon said in a rush.

Poor Tyler wasn't paranoid at all. I had inadvertently gotten Devon caught. "That's not the point is it? You always did well in school, why would you need to change your grades?"

"That school is a totalitarian regime. They control you with grades. We're freedom fighters."

He was so earnest I wanted to hug him. I stared at him instead. People are naturally inclined to fill silences.

"It's totally boring. I learn much more coding. Danny, Todd, and Ben agree with me."

"You told Danny, Todd, and Ben?" I said.

"They never did any work in middle school and it didn't hurt them. Those guys are sick coders. I don't know why they're wasting their time working for you."

"Yeah, me either. What kind of punishment is the headmaster talking about?" I said.

"Nothing yet. Their IT guy didn't keep the logs that showed our IP addresses. Total idiot. But he'll probably figure out that they're automatically backed up. And they changed their firewall configuration; now we can't get in to erase them."

"You don't feel bad at all about what you did, just about getting caught?" I said.

"Like I said, they're a . . ."

"Totalitarian regime. Yeah I got that. Look, I won't lie to you. I was bored in school too. But I need you to understand that this was not the right way to handle it. There are rules and laws for a reason. And if people broke them whenever they didn't agree with them, the world wouldn't be a very nice place."

I was prepared for an "act of conscience" debate or an argument about passive resistance. I was not prepared for him to break out in tears. I held him and let him sob. It seemed like the only time I got close to my family now was when they were crying. I felt his little shoulders shake.

"It's okay. We'll work it out," I said to him when he had caught his breath.

"The headmaster said he was going to call our parents. I told him that Mom was away, so he's going to call you."

For a moment it occurred to me that he might be playing me, but looking down at his tear-streaked face, I felt ashamed for thinking it. "I won't tell your mom until we have some time to figure out how we're going to handle this."

I earned another hug for that. I fed him a burrito and orange soda. Pratt shared his Starbursts with him. Then I drove him to the Big House and let him off around the corner to make sure Suzanne didn't see us.

"What a great kid," was how Pratt greeted me when I got back. Todd and Ben agreed enthusiastically. It was full confirmation that I was a terrible father.

"You brought my son into this? You not only risk compromising my identity, you risk his safety? I should shoot all three of you on principle," I said.

"He just showed up," Todd said.

"And we don't know his name either," Ben added.

"We have this under control," Pratt said.

"Oh, then I feel perfectly safe," I said.

They all smiled and nodded. Todd and Ben evidently didn't get sarcasm any more than Pratt did.

"I need to hear you say it. My son is off-limits from now on, understood?"

"Understood," they said in unison.

"Have you at least made any progress on finding Westfield or whatever his real name is?"

"I should have gotten a picture of him on my phone. I thought we could get something off a security camera or a satellite. He's better than I thought."

"If you had tried to pull out your phone, he would have shot you. And I expect him to be good. That's why we have to find him before he finds us. He's seen my car. There are millions of brown Camrys on the road, but if he's that good, who knows."

"We thought of that. Your registration doesn't exist," Pratt said.

"You erased my DMV records?"

"I erased you period," Pratt said.

"What do you mean "period"?"

"Social Security, credit history, birth record. Everything."

"What about my bank accounts?"

"Duh."

Todd and Ben laughed.

"I bounced an alimony check to my wife. I'm more scared of her than I am of Westfield," I said.

"He's being sarcastic," Pratt explained to Todd and Ben.

"Try coding after I cut off all your fingers," I said. "Tell me how I'm going to get money to my wife."

"Ex-wife," Caroline chimed in.

"Todd's fingers go first."

"I have your money in off-shore accounts under made-up names. At your age, you should have more saved, by the way. I can route it through some dummy accounts and into her account pretty safely," Pratt said.

"As long as it's done by tomorrow. The transfer should be for—"

"I know how much. It was in your checking records. You should send more. Devon needs a new computer," Pratt said.

"Let's let the boys work," Caroline said and dragged me into my bedroom before I strangled all three of them.

"They're good. They won't make it easy for Westfield to find your family," Caroline said.

"No more bullshit," I said. "You know he's still working on Tiresias. That's why you shot the Russian, why you made up the crew of Israelis," I said. "You wanted to buy time for Pratt to complete the program."

"The one I saved you from is as dangerous as a crew of Israelis."

"How would you know that?"

"I'm the one who took the bullet," she said.

"Your plan is to keep Pratt alive long enough to complete Tiresias and steal it for who?"

"It's not that simple," she said.

"For who?"

"For us. Me and you," she said. "How many senior citizen contractors do you know? We don't get retirement plans for a reason. We don't live long enough to collect. This is our chance."

"We sell it, and you and I sail into the sunset together. Don't you want to get down on one knee and ask me?"

"It could be fun. But even if we go our separate ways, we still need this," she said.

"And all that stuff about getting revenge on Westfield for killing Rob was a bunch of shit."

"I still want to get him, but I want to take care of myself first," she said.

"And me."

"That's the deal."

"And Pratt and his two minions?"

"They'll need to disappear. New lives, start to finish. You won't have to worry about them spilling your identity," she said.

"That's quite a plan. It would have been nice to know before all the killing, but I'm glad you decided to share it with me now."

Caroline gave me one of her blinding smiles.

"What?" I said.

"Unlike the boys, I do appreciate sarcasm. And you're cute when you're suspicious."

"It's not going to work."

"It's an excellent plan and has at least a small chance of working," she said.

"You're not going to charm me or seduce me or flatter me into letting you sell this thing, or hand it to someone who is already paying you, or do whatever else you have planned."

"I need you," she said and drew close.

"I mean it this time."

"I need you to help me pull this off. I can't do it alone."

"We're down to flattery already," I said.

"Westfield has a fleet of contractors looking for us. The Russians are after us. And a crazy Israeli. I have three code geeks. I can't keep them alive alone. I need you," she said.

"I get it," I said, suddenly weary.

"Now I mean it the other way."

"We're back to seduction?"

And then the conversation was over.

CHAPTER ELEVEN

We settled into an odd version of a domestic routine. The boys worked almost round the clock, splitting their time between working on Tiresias and trying to track down Westfield. That was the compromise Caroline and I agreed on. The boys swore that they would get to Westfield before he got to me and my family. I didn't have much choice but to trust them.

I worked on my Morons book by day and got visits from Caroline at night. Pratt managed to get my alimony payment into Suzanne's account. I did my shocked but concerned parent routine when the headmaster called and assured him that Devon would never break school rules. He told me that they would be investigating further, but days went by and I didn't hear from him.

The only time I left the house was to get my poor Camry taken care of. I wanted Lino to change the paint job. As anonymous as my car was, if Westfield scanned enough security camera footage, he could get lucky.

I always felt ridiculous in my disguise. It wasn't what an undercover cop looked like. It was like the movie version that Lino would believe they would look like. As it turned out, it saved my life.

Westfield must have been following up on every brown Camry in the tri-state area. His contractors were set up inside his shop when I pulled in. Lino came running out to greet me, which immediately set off my internal alarm. The guy usually had the classic mechanic's saunter, like he was grudgingly coming out to see what kind of mess you'd made of his work now.

I guess their plan was for him to get me inside and get a better look at me. He told me he wanted to show me all the shades of gray paint I could choose from. He made it sound like he gave a shit, which was another giveaway. And when we got close to the shop, I could see it looked empty, which was strike three. Lino put most sweatshops to shame in how hard he worked his crew.

"How many of them are they?" I said to him with a smile and laughed as if I had told him a joke.

"How many of who?" which confirmed my suspicions. His normal response would have been something along the lines of, "What the fuck are you talking about?"

"They probably gave you a bunch of shit about national security. They work for a drug dealer I put away. Act like you're telling me a joke back, and tell me how many there are and where they're set up."

Lino hesitated. I could almost smell the brain cells he was burning trying to figure this out. "If we walk into that shop, you get killed in the crossfire along with me," I said.

"Two guys, one on each side. They told me you were some kind of terrorist," he spat out.

"Now laugh," I said.

His fake guffaw was pathetic, but it made me laugh too, so it worked.

If they'd been smart, these clowns would have grabbed me as soon as I got out of my car. But they were well-armed clowns and if they managed to shoot me in the head, it would have still made me just as dead.

"You're going to tell them I went into your office to take a dump. And if you fuck this up, Lino, I'm going to find you and take you apart piece by piece with your own tools." I gave him another good fake laugh to cover the fact that he turned sheet white.

Lino walked into the shop like he was going to the firing squad. I detoured into his office. Minutes later two oversized muscle heads rushed in and kicked down the bathroom door. It would have been fun to see the perplexed look on their faces when they saw it was empty. I stood up from behind Lino's desk with my Browning out.

This was different from when I had tried to subdue the Suit. When you are facing two adversaries, the right thing to do is shoot them, not talk to them, period. If they turn and fire at the same time, it's hard to hit them both before one of them gets a shot off. But I wanted at least one of them alive, and I knew they weren't trained nearly as well as the Suit.

"Drop your guns and turn slowly, and you won't die in a service station men's room," I said.

The one on the left whirled with his gun extended. I shot him in the head. The other one froze.

"Your partner didn't know how to follow instructions. What's the lesson of the day?" I said.

The one on the right dropped his gun and turned around like he was in slow motion.

"At least one of you is a fast learner."

Lino came into his office, saw the dead guy and puked.

"You're closed for the day. Lock up and leave me the key."

Seeing dead people encourages cooperation. Lino had the place closed up in record time. I sent him on his way with a warning not to talk about anything he saw. He looked like he took it to heart.

A body shop turns out to be a pretty good place to conduct an interrogation. I felt stupid for not using it before. I fastened the contractor's feet to the tracks on the garage floor and his hands to the lift. A push of a button and I had a hydraulic version of the rack.

"Who hired you?"

No answer.

I pushed the button. The contractor screamed in pain. It wouldn't take long.

"I thought you were the fast learner. Should I ask again?"

No answer.

I pushed the button. I could hear his shoulders dislocate with a pop. His scream was higher pitched now. I gave him time to live with the pain.

I moved my finger slowly toward the button.

"I don't know. They use an anonymous drop."

"How did they recruit you?"

"Contacted me through a chat room. A lot of ex-military use it."

"Why you?"

"I applied to the CIA over a year ago. They dinged me. Then they came back and said my country needed me. They knew everything I'd put in my application, that's how I knew it was legit."

"What's your mission?"

This was the key question and we both knew it. He hadn't told me anything yet. This was crossing a different line. He was in a lot of pain. I respected that he hesitated. I didn't want to hit the button again. He was close to passing out.

"I haven't done any permanent damage yet. The next time I hit the button, you'll have to pay someone to help you jerk off."

I moved my hand toward the button.

"Grab the kid. Kill you. Kill the Israeli."

"Why the Israeli?"

As a rule, we try not to kill our allies' agents unless we have to. What had the Suit done to merit termination?

"Why were you supposed to kill the Israeli?"

I realized I wasn't going to get an answer. The contractor had passed out from the pain.

I cut him down and dumped him in the passenger seat of one of the cars in Lino's lot. I was unlikely to get more out of him and the longer I stayed at Lino's the bigger the risk. The smart move would have been to kill him, but he had only seen me in disguise, and with shock setting in, he wouldn't be able to tell Westfield much. It did mean that I could never go back to Lino's, which was a shame.

I dragged the dead contractor to the car and sat him on his buddy's lap. I drove them to a deserted lot. I called 9-1-1 on a burner cellphone, which I dropped at the scene, and sprinted back to Lino's. I got in the Camry and headed home.

I called Pratt on a secure cell on the way. He and Caroline each had one. Pratt had set them up. He changed the encryption every time we used them. "I need you to erase the satellite and security cameras between the garage and home," I said.

"Okay. Caroline wants to talk to you."

That was it from the kid. No questions.

"What happened?" Caroline asked.

"Ambush. I handled it. Got one of them alive."

"Anything good?"

"He said they want to kill the Israeli. Does that mean anything to you?"

"Nope. We shouldn't stay on. No matter how good Pratt says his encryption is."

"I'm on my way home," I said.

"See you soon," she said.

It was almost like we were a normal couple.

"Honey, I'm home," I bellowed when I arrived home.

The house was empty. At first, I had the weird feeling that they were all going to jump out and yell surprise. I looked in every room. I was exasperated that they had ignored my warning about not going out. I called Pratt's phone and heard it ring from the living room. His and Caroline's phones were sitting side by side on the coffee table. Next to them, there were two messages, written in lipstick on the table. The first said, "Thanks for everything," and was signed Danny Pratt. Like if he had only signed Danny, I wouldn't know who it was from. The second was from Caroline. "I got the boys out without compromising your identity. I'm sorry it had to end this way. *L'Chaim.*"

"The worst kind of fool is the one who fools himself," Nachash murmured in my head.

And of course, he was right. I had convinced myself that we had common cause and that keeping her close was the best way to figure out what she was up to. And she had literally shouted the answer at me. The contractors had been ordered to kill the Israeli. It wasn't the Suit they were after. It was Caroline.

It was a classic strategy. The Suit worked the outside and she worked the inside. I had to give her credit for her commitment.

Sex was one thing, but taking a bullet to gain my confidence was hard-core.

I still should have figured it out. When she was hurt and semi-delirious she had yelled, "*Tchaaaa.*" I thought it was a foreign curse that I didn't know, but she had been slurring her words. She was saying, "chara," the same as the Suit had. I had made the classic counterespionage mistake. I had believed what I wanted to.

My cell phone rang and for a moment I thought it might be her. It was the headmaster at Devon's school. He wanted to know if I could be in his office in half an hour. Why not, I thought. I had no idea what I was going to do next anyway.

Suzanne was already seated in his office when I got there. Two other sets of parents, presumably belonging to Devon's partners in crime, were there as well. Suzanne glared at me either because I was the last to arrive or just because. The only good news was that there was no sign of Rowan.

"Thank you all for coming in on such short notice. We have had a disturbing development in the hacking issue with your children," the headmaster said.

He let this hang in the air for a moment. It was a typical interrogation technique. The subject becomes uncomfortable enough to blurt something out and fill the silence. I pre-empted any blurting. If the boys had done something else that they could get in trouble for, I didn't want one of their parents spitting out a confession.

"What kind of development?" I said. Turning the question around was also textbook.

"As you know, this is a very serious situation. Your sons are suspected of hacking into the school servers and changing grades," the headmaster said, looking from parent to parent.

He said "suspected," which was a good sign. And he didn't offer any new information. Were his IT guys having a hard time using the server logs to nail the boys? The other parents looked puzzled and nervous, which meant they didn't know anything either.

One of the dads started to speak. I interrupted. "Yes and we are all very concerned. What more can you tell us about this awful accusation?"

If the headmaster had a weapon, I would have regretted not wearing my vest. As it was, all he could do was stare daggers. *Staring Daggers*, that actually would have been a funny chapter name for my *Stabbing Weapons for Morons* books.

"Someone has hacked into the servers again and erased the backup logs. We questioned your sons about it earlier this afternoon and they denied it, but who else would have the skill and the motive to do this kind of thing?"

"I don't mean to be naïve, but are our sons the only computer literate students at the school?"

"Of course not. We have an excellent computer science program," the headmaster said.

"Then it would seem there would be any number of students with the skills to do this." I escalated the tempo of the conversation, to put the headmaster on the defensive.

"Our IT group set up extremely powerful security to prevent that."

"It would seem unlikely that our seventh graders could have the skills to circumvent them, wouldn't it?" I said.

"They had the skills to hack into the servers to begin with. I don't know what they're capable of."

He had made a mistake and he knew it. I waited to let it sink in. "So your position is that our sons had to have hacked into the servers, which there is no proof of, because they hacked into the servers again and erased the logs. But your only reason for believing that they could have erased the logs is that they hacked into the servers in the first place. It's been a long time since I was in school, but they used to call that circular logic."

"I hope you aren't trying to make light of this, because this is a very serious situation," the headmaster said, his tone rising.

"On the contrary. I take this very seriously. I only consented to taking this meeting without my lawyer because my wife insisted. I had assumed that this school would not level accusations that our boys committed an act worthy of expulsion unless it had incontrovertible proof. Now I am finding out that there are only suspicions and baseless inferences. Your IT staff has serious issues if they have allowed your servers to be hacked a second time despite what you describe as extremely powerful security measures. It sounds like your issue is with them, not with us and not with our sons."

I had hit all the bases: lawyers, false accusations, incompetence. Now we would see how much belly he had for a fight.

"We take our honor code here very seriously. We are obligated to pursue any and all breaches aggressively. I hope you can appreciate that," he said.

"That's one of the things that makes this such a great school. And why we feel lucky to have our sons as part of it," I said, accepting his surrender.

"Well then, thank you for coming in. I will keep you apprised of any further developments," was his final capitulation.

"Thank *you*," I said, and stood up and shook his hand. I ush-ered Suzanne and the other parents out before anyone could say anything stupid.

"That was weird," one of the mothers said.

"What he said was slander. Maybe we should sue him," the father added.

"Maybe we should go home," I said.

I took Suzanne by the hand and led the way out. I was encour-aged that she let me.

"I might have a shot at PTA president," I said to her when we were outside.

She pulled her hand loose. "How did the boys erase the logs?"

"I have no idea. It sounded pretty complicated."

"You see, I don't know if you're telling me the truth or manip-ulating me like you did the headmaster."

"I kept our son from possibly getting expelled. How does that make me a bad guy?" I said.

"Because you twist things like it's second nature. I'm not sure if you know when you're doing it anymore. I certainly don't."

"I want the best for you and Devon. That's all I care about. And you know that's not a lie," I said.

"I look back at our marriage now, and I don't know what was real and what wasn't. I don't know what parts of you are real. Did you become this way, or is this who you've always been and I couldn't tell because you're such a good liar? And I'm afraid that our son is turning into one too."

And then she was gone. What was I doing wrong that everyone was leaving me? With Caroline I was too honest, and with Suzanne I wasn't honest enough. Whatever I did, the result was the same.

I drove back home and found a large man peering through the front window. I jumped out of the car. As he turned, I delivered a flat-handed blow to his solar plexus. It was the same blow I had given Rob and it had the same effect. Connor fell to the ground, gasping for breath.

"Who do you work for?" I screamed at him.

It was a useless question. Connor couldn't breathe much less speak, but I yelled it again. "Who do you work for?!"

It seemed to make perfect sense. Who better to keep tabs on me than Connor? He had the ideal excuse to check up on me. And he kept stopping by like a sitcom character making his comic entrance. I should have seen it before.

I pressed my elbow right below his Adam's apple. With the right amount of force it feels like you're going to suffocate. It's not waterboarding, but it gives some of the same feeling.

"You have one more chance before I crush your larynx. Who sent you?"

I reduced the pressure enough for him to wheeze a response.

"Needed last chapter. Didn't return my calls."

I looked down at Connor lying on my lawn like a fat fish struggling for air. He was no agent. If he were, he would have moved on me long before now. I had lost my professional distance. If I wrote about it for Connor it would have been called *How to Get Killed for Morons*. But seeing the look on his face, I doubted I would be writing any more for him. He struggled to his feet.

"It's okay. We can skip the last chapter. It works as it is," he croaked. "I'll have your check to you tomorrow."

"Make it out to cash."

I didn't try to make an excuse or apologize. I could see there was no point. I sat down on the front steps and watched him get in his car and drive away. I sat there a long time. I don't know how long. Caroline and the Israelis could have agents on the way to kill me, and it would be as easy as target practice. And I didn't care. Until Devon showed up.

"Hey Dad, are you waiting for someone?"

"Yes. It's about time you got here," I said. It felt good to see the 'boy are your jokes stupid' look on his face. "Let's get some Taco Bell," I said.

We drove to Central Avenue and sat in the back. Taco Bell is much better as take-out food. Being there ruins the illusion that you are eating real food. It didn't seem to bother Devon.

"How are things going at school?" was my opener. Not imaginative, but I didn't want to dive right in.

"It sucks, as usual."

"How about soccer? I'm sorry I missed the last couple of games. Mom says you're getting the hang of it."

"Soccer sucks worse than school. Where are Danny and the guys?"

"They have another job to do. They won't be around for a while."

"I want Danny to show me how he erased the server logs. He's the one who did it, right?"

"You know that's not the lesson I'm hoping you learned from this, right?"

"School is all jerkoff teachers and douchey rich kids. I learned more from hacking into the school servers than I ever learned at school."

Hearing my sweet little Devon say words like "jerkoff" and "douchey" almost made me cry. "The other day, you told me you're not a little kid anymore. You're right. Here's the hard truth. You keep doing stuff like that and you will get caught. And next time there won't be anyone to bail you out. Then what? You get expelled? If that's what you want, I'll save you the trouble and we can put you back in public school right now."

"I told you, I'm not going back to public prison."

"Then get your act together and stop doing stupid shit. Danny Pratt went to MIT. He didn't get there by getting expelled from middle school. You and your buddies can spend as much time coding as you want, and make fun of the other kids and the teachers behind their backs, but you get your homework done and you don't get into any more trouble, or I will send you back to public school whether you like it or not." I held my breath. I thought there was a good chance that he would break out in tears or get up and leave.

"Okay. But I want a new computer. Mine's two years old and it sucks ass."

Part of me mourned the little boy who I could see was gone, and part of me was proud of Devon for driving a good bargain.

"Deal. But you show me a month of good behavior first."

"Deal," Devon said and held out his hand.

We shook as if commemorating the moment that our relationship had changed forever. Nachash was wrong. Devon was much stronger than I was at his age. For the first time in a while, I felt like he would be okay.

CHAPTER TWELVE

slept in the Camry behind the local supermarket. I didn't want to make it too easy for the Suit and Caroline. I didn't see any sign of them the next morning on my home monitoring app. I did see Connor personally drop off my check. I had never seen him move so fast. I gathered the supplies I needed and headed out.

I checked the tracker app on my phone and was surprised to find that the dot I had placed on Pratt's computer was still active. Caroline was so confident that she had me in her thrall that she hadn't thought to check. I didn't relish the thought of killing her, but she was right, Tiresias was the key. I needed it to make a deal with Westfield. That was the only way to keep my family safe and that was all that mattered.

I stopped at the bank and cashed my check. I had only one more stop to make. I pulled into a shiny new parking garage under a chrome and glass office building. The doctors' offices were on the top floor. They looked more like lawyers' offices. Rowan's waiting room was packed. His receptionist was young and pretty and bore no resemblance to Mrs. Levine, but she had the same suspicious attitude.

"Can I help you?"

"I need to have a quick word with Dr. Rowan."

"Do you have an appointment?"

"Tell him Gib Alexander needs to speak with him. It's an emergency."

"I'm sorry, but . . ."

I leaned in close when I interrupted her. This job means a lot of role-playing. It didn't come naturally to me, but I had learned from long practice. Maybe if I had been better at it, I would still be married. There was the perfect amount of crazy in my eyes. "Get him," was all I said.

The receptionist got up and hurried to the back. She returned quickly and ushered me into Rowan's consultation room. Rowan got up to shake my hand.

"Is everything all right with Suzanne?"

I shook his hand and didn't let go. "We need to have a quick chat." He tried to withdraw his hand, but I held on. "I could tell you not to see Suzanne anymore, but that wouldn't be fair to her. She's an adult and has the right to make her own mistakes," I said.

"Have you been drinking or something? You should go before you make a big mistake." He tried to pull away again and seemed befuddled that he wasn't able to break my grip. "You can't come into my office and . . ."

I cut him off. "Devon's a different story. You're going to tell him that he doesn't seem happy playing soccer and that it's okay with you if he quits. And you're going to make Suzanne believe it too."

"I can see you're upset and I'm trying to be patient here, but . . ." He tried to sucker punch me in mid-sentence with his free hand. Even without my training I would have seen it coming. I blocked his looping roundhouse punch with my elbow. The point of the elbow hit the underside of his funny bone. He howled in pain and his arm fell limply to his side.

"Your arm feels numb. That will go away in a couple of hours."
I slapped an envelope on his desk. "That has my next three months'
alimony payments in it. Put it in Suzanne's mailbox. I'll know if
you don't. And have the talk with Devon tonight."

"Who the fuck do you think you are? I'll have my lawyer take
away your house and whatever savings you have stuffed under your
mattress," he said.

"Considering you swung at me, you wouldn't have a very good
case. Plus, Suzanne wouldn't be too happy with you trying to take
money from the person who supports her. And perhaps most
important, I would find you and do enough nerve damage to your
arms that your days of being a high-priced quack would be over."
I let go of his hand. He grabbed his limp arm and massaged it. A
decent chiropractor should be able to do better than that. "And I'm
Devon's father. That's who the fuck I am," I said.

It would take Rowan a while to process what had happened.
It's confusing when you have to reevaluate someone. But he would
do what I asked. He liked his cushy life. Some part of him might
whisper that I was bluffing, but he had too much to lose.

Back in the Camry my mind was clear. I followed the tracking
dot and didn't dwell on what would happen next. I couldn't plan,
because I didn't have any information about where they were. All I
could do was regain my professional calm and be ready to do what
was necessary. "A calm mind is an open mind," Nachash whispered.

I didn't have to go far to find them. They were holed up about
thirty minutes north in Croton. The house was set back from the
street on a three-acre corner lot. It was bordered on one side by a
nature preserve and the other side by a lot that was surrounded by
high wooden fences. The house itself was a three-story Georgian

with brick walls and sight lines across the property. With enough firepower, you could defend it against a platoon.

It was listed as being owned by Silicon Works, a corporation registered in Delaware and doing business in New York State, address unspecified. The Israelis would have bought the house with the fiction that clients and workers from overseas were housed here on a temporary basis. Everything would be handled online and done through a web of shell companies. None of it would stand up to too much scrutiny, but as long as they paid their taxes on time, no one was likely to look. And if they did look, the companies and the accounts would quickly shut down and the trail would be dead.

I stashed my car and camped out in the woods. For camouflage work, I use my own version of the MOLLE system. Armed forces love acronyms almost as much as the agencies love medical metaphors. This one stands for "modular lightweight load carrying equipment." It's the camouflage gear you imagine when you envision soldiers in the woods, colored to blend in and full of pouches and attachments. There are a bunch of newer systems used now, but I'm loyal to MOLLE. It held my Remington MSR, my Browning, grenades, flares, binoculars, night vision goggles, tablet computer, surveillance equipment, water, rations, and all the other fun stuff you might need for this kind of job without getting too bulky to move. For my camo clothes, I used a new digital design instead of the old three-color model. It's supposed to blend in better. I don't like change, but I do like new toys.

I set up in a thicket that provided natural cover. It was going to be a long watch-and-wait. I needed to know who was inside and where they were set up. Were they patrolling the grounds? Did they go into the woods? Was anything coming in or going out? I couldn't be sure of any of it unless I put in the time. Surprisingly my germophobia doesn't bother me much in the woods. I can't say I enjoy being out in nature, but it seems clean somehow.

I did my breathing exercises. I needed to be alert, but you can't sustain intense vigilance over long periods. You need to find a relaxed state where you notice anything that changes but you keep your adrenaline at bay. Otherwise you lose focus, your body cramps, and you miss things that can get you killed. It's a little like meditation. You know you are going to get random thoughts coming into your head. The key is not to fight them. You recognize them, accept them, and then refocus on your surveillance. Nachash was a master at it. He could beat a statue in a staring contest, but if a fly moved in his field of vision, he could grab it without missing a breath.

It comes much harder for me. Nachash always said that my mind was way too busy. I used to tell him his mouth was too busy. How had he let Westfield's B list contractors get to him? And how did Westfield know about him? And had it even been Westfield? Had the Israelis seen Nachash as a threat? It made more sense that they could have gotten to him, but why? Had Nachash recruited me for Rob? He had denied it again and again, but if they were connected, then he had almost certainly lied to me. That may sound simple, but it isn't. Nachash always told me the truth. He felt it was the basis of the student–teacher relationship—absolute unvarnished truth. He often refused to answer me, but he never lied. And I didn't hold back with him. There were times that I hated him and told him so, and he never blinked. It was the only relationship in my life where I never had to think before I spoke.

Maybe that's why I still spoke to him in my head. I could see him nodding with that maddening tight-lipped smile of his and flipped him the bird in my mind. It's not nice to gloat.

A van with Good Guys Home Security emblazoned on the side pulled up in front of the house. This type of local security usually cruises around the neighborhood. Why was this one stopping? Two hundred and twenty-five pounds of rent-a-cop squeezed into a two hundred pound bag of a blue uniform emerged from the van and headed toward the woods. He didn't look happy. Exercise was clearly not his favorite part of the job. My guess was that he had to check off the woods as part of his daily rounds.

The rent-a-cop lumbered up to the tree line, peered into the woods, nodded to himself, and lumbered back to his car. Whatever the town was paying Good Guys Home Security, they weren't getting their money's worth. Then again, the odds of any serious mischief happening in a suburban nature preserve were small and the rent-a-cop knew that.

That was the big excitement for the next twenty-four hours. At night, the whole property lit up with floodlights, no advantage to be gained there. Nothing moved. I got no sleep and ate three MREs. Officially, it stands for "meals ready to eat." Unofficially, soldiers call it "meals rejected by everyone," or "meals ready to excrete" among other even less appetizing names. It's sort of like airplane food jammed into little packets. Some come with an FRH, "flame ration heater"—they do love acronyms—that use an exothermic reaction to produce enough heat to warm them up. But heating this crap up doesn't make it taste much better. They're easy to transport, are nutritionally sound, and don't open accidentally under pressure, but they taste like feet. I don't know for sure that the army makes them taste terrible to make their troops more ornery, but it certainly works that way.

Lying in a bush and staring at a suburban McMansion was not what I had envisioned when Rob had first recruited me. It was supposed to be about getting the bad guys and making the world a safer place. I had just started dating Suzanne and I already knew where I wanted things to go. Looking back, I think I wanted to feel worthy of her. I wasn't going to be a surgeon and I was never going to write the great American novel. Saving the world seemed like a good backup. I wish I could tell her, "I know you think I'm holding back from you, but it's only because I wanted to be a hero to deserve you." Pratt would have loved the irony.

I wanted to make a move. I knew I should be patient, but I could feel Westfield's minions closing in on my family.

"That is why we separate our lives," Nachash admonished me.

"It's a little too late for that, but thanks."

Nachash didn't have any more appreciation for sarcasm than Pratt did.

My guess was that the Suit and Caroline were alone. I killed the Suit's partner and they brought in Caroline. It was risky for Israel to have too many agents operating on American soil. If they got caught, it would cause a major issue with their most important ally. And they almost never use contractors. They don't trust anyone they didn't train themselves.

"Professionals do not guess," Nachash reminded me unhelpfully.

"It's an educated guess."

"Educated enough to risk your life?"

"Enough to try to keep my family safe," I said. "And he who dares wins." It was my trump card, Nachash's favorite saying. It came from the Israeli Special Forces, but U.S. Special Forces had adopted it too. "And you're not here, so I get the last word for a change."

I pulled out my tablet. Pratt had set it up so it was untraceable. The house's router was secure and would be hard to crack, but the neighbors weren't. I connected and used Google Voice to call Good Guy Security.

"I live next door to 143 Cedar Place. There's a strange woman in the house with a group of men doing unspeakable things. This is a family neighborhood. And it looks like someone is going to get hurt. I tried 911 but they put me on hold. I need you to get someone over here right now."

"What kind of activity are you seeing, please?"

"There are whips and chains, and I see blood."

"We can't get involved in domestic situations sir.'

"These don't look like the owners of the house. What do we pay you people for if not to keep us safe? You need to send someone right now," I yelled and hung up.

I had put the Good Guys in a bad position. I sounded like a crackpot, so they wouldn't want to call the police and look foolish, but crackpot or not, angry neighbors can turn up at neighborhood association meetings and get security companies fired. Their guy would be nearby if he kept the same daily schedule. They would radio him to check it out.

I didn't want the cops showing up, because it could turn into a blood bath. The plus-sized rent-a-cop was more predictable. Caroline would answer the door. She was the one more suited to smile him into going away. The Suit would stay with the boys to make sure they didn't do anything stupid. If I was right and there were only the two of them, the backdoor would be unguarded. I left my MOLLE in the thicket. I took only my Browning and a belt pack with my surveillance equipment and a few other goodies. I moved quietly through the woods to where the tree line was closest to the back door.

I was barely in place when the rent-a-cop arrived in the Good Guy van. He approached the front door with a determined waddle. Caroline and the Suit would have seen him make his rounds enough times that they wouldn't shoot him on sight. He rang the doorbell and waited. Caroline answered. I couldn't hear what they were saying, but the conversation would go something like this, "I'm with Good Guy Security. We got a call about an incident with this residence. Is the owner at home?"

"I'm the owner. Well, my company is. I'm with Silicon Works and we own the house. What kind of incident could there possibly be?" Caroline would ask and flash that hypnotic smile.

The rent-a-cop would swallow hard and stutter, "Well, your neighbor called and said that there was, um, well, I'd like to take a look inside to make sure everything is okay, if that's all right with you."

"I don't mean to be difficult, but the house is a mess, and I would be terribly embarrassed to have you see it that way," with another smile.

"Okay, then can you at least have the other fellows staying with you come to the door?" the rent-a-cop would ask.

"I have only one fellow with me and he's busy working right now. Maybe I should call your supervisor and discuss the situation with him?" she was turning indignant.

If the rent-a-cop didn't go away then, the Suit would come to the door. "Is there a problem here? I'm trying to get my work done and I am on a very tight deadline."

That would do it for the rent-a-cop. He would mumble an inarticulate apology and stage a clumsy retreat. I estimated the whole thing would take about four minutes. That's how long I would have to get to the back door, get it open, and find a hiding place. I sprinted full out. The run was too long not to attract attention. If there were someone guarding the back door, they would hit me no matter how careful I was.

The lock on the back door was a high-end dead bolt. I didn't try my lock picking tools. I sprayed lubricant into the lock and inserted a tiny, power drill. It bore through the tumblers in less than a minute. It had a silencer and made almost no noise. I slipped in a screwdriver, turned, and was in.

I started in the kitchen. I stuck a tiny webcam under the refrigerator, moved into the dining room and stuck a webcam under the table. I went back through the kitchen into the hall. I stuck a webcam under the frame of a Monet lithograph that hung on the wall. Now I needed to hide.

I quietly opened a door and found a bathroom. That wasn't a good idea. I heard the front door close. I was running out of time. I opened another door and found a closet full of coats. I had one more try before whoever had answered the door came down the hall. The last door did the trick. I closed it behind me and descended into the basement.

I lit a glowstick and looked around. It wasn't your average finished basement. It had multiple interrogation chairs with electronically controlled metal restraints capable of exerting variable pressure, some imaginative tools both sharp and dull, and a variety of drugs and syringes. It wouldn't be needed for the boys, which meant I wasn't in immediate danger of discovery, but Caroline or the Suit would find the drilled lock in the back soon enough. The clock was ticking.

I slipped on my glasses, and the Bluetooth earpiece in case I could pick up any stray audio. I toggled between the feeds from the webcams I had set up. The kitchen and dining room were empty. I caught a glimpse of Caroline going upstairs from the webcam in the picture frame, which meant she had charmed the rent-a-cop all by herself. The poor guy would probably be dreaming about her for weeks.

She was probably watching the boys, and the Suit was watching the property. That would likely put her on the second floor and him on the third floor. Assuming it was only the two of them, I would take out the Suit first. Getting past Caroline on the second floor was risky, but if I went right after her, I risked catching Pratt and the boys in a crossfire, and I had to admit that I didn't like the idea of killing her. With the Suit dead, I might be able to negotiate.

As I started up the basement stairs, my webcam picked up Pratt walking into the kitchen. The kid's endless appetite had finally come in handy. He was staring at the open refrigerator with a forlorn expression on his face. Most safe houses aren't stocked with candy and orange soda.

"You shouldn't have left. My snacks were better," I said.

He turned calmly as if he weren't the least surprised to see me. "I wasn't given much of a choice. You used the microdot to track us?"

"When did you find it?"

"About 30 seconds after you planted it. I was one of the guys who wrote the NSA software that jams those things."

"You wanted me to find you."

"Caroline said you were going to stop us from releasing Tiresias. That's why she had to get us away from you. I didn't believe her."

"Why?"

"I knew she was manipulating me. You weren't. She was watching me too carefully to contact you directly, but I made sure she didn't find the tracking dot," he said.

"She's Israeli, probably Mossad. She has no interest in letting you release Tiresias."

I could see Pratt digest this. His brain told him it made sense. His heart didn't want to listen.

"Who else is with her?" I asked.

"Just this guy she calls Richard."

The Suit didn't look like a Richard. He was more like a Trent or Brett. Then again, his real name was probably something like Eitan or Ori.

"Tell her you can't work unless you have Starburst and orange soda. We need to get her out of the house. Richard will want to tell you to shut up and work, but she'll do it if you pitch enough of a fit," I said.

"I don't pitch fits. She'll know I'm faking."

"Be persistent. You're good at persistence." I heard movement on the stairs. "Do it quickly, we don't have much time," I said and hurried back to the basement.

The webcam on the picture frame gave me a good view of Caroline walking down the hall, and the webcam in the kitchen picked her up after that. She had Pratt on a tight leash. That was no surprise. She'd had me on one too. It would make a good *Dr. Phil* show, "Spies Who Love Too Much and the Women Who Hurt Them." Of course, any professional who actually went on a show like that would be discreetly disposed of, but it would get good ratings.

"Your friends upstairs need you. They don't make any progress without you," I heard Caroline say to Pratt.

"I need orange soda and Starburst. I'm going through withdrawal."

"We don't have time for snack runs," Caroline said.

"I have a headache that feels like my cerebellum is imploding. If I don't get a big sugar fix, I can't code."

"Are you going to let Todd and Ben do this by themselves? This is your baby."

This was a nice appeal to his ego, but it was the wrong move. It was too obviously a manipulation.

"They can't do it by themselves. You said it yourself. Do you have to ask Richard's permission?" Pratt asked with studied innocence.

Caroline seemed genuinely annoyed by the idea that she might need his permission. Was there friction between her and the Suit? How could I exploit it?

She put a hand on his shoulder and gave him one of her best high-wattage smiles.

"Go upstairs and tell Richard I went for supplies. Will you do your best to keep things moving while I'm gone?"

Pratt nodded like he meant it. He probably did. If she had done that to me, I would have gone upstairs and tried to do some coding too. That or had sex with her on the kitchen floor.

I heard footsteps pounding down the stairs. I heard the front door fling open and then slam shut. The Suit was not happy about Caroline's departure. I saw him come down the hall and into the kitchen. He pulled a beer out of the refrigerator. His Desert Eagle was in a shoulder holster. It was a better opportunity than I could have hoped for. He was away from the boys and he was preoccupied.

I eased myself through the basement door and moved quietly toward the kitchen. The Suit scanned the backyard. He caught the drilled lock and went to examine it. I have no issues with shooting someone in the back. It's not gallant or the way they would do it in the movies, but it's a great way to stay alive. And he would do the same to me.

My webcam glitched and I froze. Then it straightened itself out. The Suit hadn't moved. I charged into the kitchen with my Browning in front of me, and everything went dark.

CHAPTER THIRTEEN

The world went from black to bright white in what felt like an instant. My head hurt. My senses returned slowly. I tried to move my arms and legs but no luck. I was in the basement confined in an interrogation chair looking into a bright white light.

"You are awake now. Good. It is time for us to talk."

I couldn't see the Suit, but I could imagine the shark smile he was wearing.

"You figured out a way to feed back a loop of the last image the webcam saw."

"It is a new piece of tech. I thought you would be too smart to go for it, but I prepared in case."

It was practically the same trick I had used at Advanced Crypto. I should have seen it coming. I gave Nachash a dirty look in my head. All those cryptic warnings, and no warning about this?

"You knew I'd track Pratt here," I said.

"Of course," he said.

"I don't know anything that will help you and I wouldn't give it to you if I did."

"You Americans are always optimistic. Live surrounded by people who want to kill you and then tell me what you will and won't do."

"I spend most of my time with people who want to kill me, and I've never been accused of being an optimist."

He gave me a laugh that was more like an angry bark. I had the feeling his bite was worse. "I would like to continue our talk, but I have matters to attend to. I will return soon, and then we will see what each of us is willing to do."

Dread is a powerful motivator. You leave the subject to stew in his own fears, and he is much easier to break when you return. But it takes time, which meant the boys weren't done programming yet. The Suit didn't want to risk trying to get Pratt out of the country before he had the program in hand.

I heard footsteps come down the stairs. It wouldn't be the Suit, and he wouldn't let Pratt or the boys out of his sight. The bright light went off, and Caroline appeared.

"I didn't take Richard for the good cop/bad cop type," I said.

"He doesn't know I'm down here."

"Which is what the good cop would say."

"I'm sorry it ended up this way," she said.

"I've told you everything I know. You won already. You don't have to keep up the act."

"It wasn't an act. Not all of it," she said.

"Tell me one thing you told me that was true."

"I do have an asshole ex-husband."

"He couldn't understand the job?"

"That is the one thing he does understand."

"Mr. Personality is your ex?" It hurt just to say it.

"I told you he was an asshole," she said.

"He let you take a bullet from his own gun to make your cover. That is some cold blood," I said.

"I took the bullet because I didn't want him to kill you."

"So let me go. Or did you change your mind?"

"I wish I could."

"You still haven't told me what he did to hurt you?" I said. I was stalling. Trying to figure out how I could use her to get free. And I couldn't help it, I wanted to know.

"He was my supervisor. I was on a mission and he pulled the plug on me. Sent in someone to take over. It set my career back years."

"Maybe he was worried about you."

"He was worried about himself. If I succeeded, he felt threatened, and if I didn't, it made him look bad," she said.

"Now you parachuted in on his mission. You both have a thing about revenge."

"Listen, he gets crazy jealous. Play to that. You might be able to get him to kill you quickly. He has a bad temper, but he's not stupid. You'll have to be subtle." She gave me a quick kiss on the lips. "That's another true thing. When I kissed you, I meant it." She flipped the light back on and turned to go. It was literally the kiss of death.

"Do me one favor," I said, and heard her pause. "Tell Pratt I'm sorry I left him in the dark. I turned out to be inferior after all."

"I don't . . ."

"Promise me. I care about the kid. I don't want to just disappear on him."

I didn't know if she heard me. All I knew was that she was gone. I pulled against the hand and foot restraints, but the metal was new and had no give to it. I closed my eyes and visualized the room. The table with the interrogation tools was in the middle. There was a chair on either side. The Suit would be down soon to start the game. Some light pain to start. He would have his gun holstered. If I could get free, I had to neutralize that first.

I counted slowly in my head to keep the dread at bay and to have some sense of time. I had only passed 900 when I heard the Suit's heavy footsteps coming down the stairs. It wasn't long enough.

"Let us start our conversation," he said.

I could hear him picking something up from the table. The sound came from directly in front of me, which told me which chair I was in. He put his hand in front of the light. It held a *lingchi* knife. I had thought about writing a chapter on it for my *Stabbing Weapons for Morons* book, but thought it was too gruesome even for the morons.

Lingchi translates as "the lingering death or death by a thousand cuts." The idea was to surgically slice off parts of the body, one by one, while still keeping the subject alive. It could be performed with any knife, but this one had a wickedly sharp edge and the Chinese characters that announced its intentions.

"I'm ready to chat. What would you like to talk about?" I said. I needed to play for time.

"I thought you were dead set on giving me nothing."

"The dead part might have been a bit exaggerated."

"Who tipped off the Russians about Tiresias?" This was a test. He knew the answer.

"Can't we start with something easier? Game shows always begin with the simple questions so you can build momentum."

He stepped into the light and placed the point of the knife surgically close to my right eye.

"Westfield, or whatever his real name is, tipped them." The two people who knew about Pratt first were Rob and Westfield. One of them had likely tipped the Russians for them to have been on the scene that quickly. Westfield made the most sense. Rob wanted to protect Pratt. Westfield needed time to assemble his team of B-list contractors. The Russians were a quick fix and gave him plausible deniability.

The Suit withdrew the knife about a millimeter. I had guessed right. "Caroline said you were stronger than this," he said.

"Sorry to disappoint you. My ex-wife feels the same way."

"You will find it less humorous when you have only one eye," he said and moved the knife to within an eyelash of my pupil. "Who tipped *us?*"

This was another test. I waited to give my answer for as long as I could and still avoid his plunging the knife into my eye. "It was my supervisor, Shrink."

"Why would he do that?"

Another good guess. I had convinced him that I was answering truthfully. Now he wanted to know Shrink's true motivation. I needed it to sound plausible. And I needed to play for time. I drew it out again, looking like I was thinking hard.

"He recruited Pratt. He didn't want him renditioned. If you and the Russians were in the game, it bought him time to make his case." It was probably close to the truth. Rob didn't want to leave me alone against the Russians. Bringing in the Israelis helped neutralize them.

"I don't believe you," he said.

"Rob's dead. I have no reason to lie."

"You have many reasons. And this was far too easy," he said.

"Maybe for you. I'm working my ass off here."

I saw his hand tense. He wanted a good grip as he shoved the knife into my eye. He would pull his hand back slightly to gather momentum and then my eye would be gone.

"Caroline knows it's true. She got it out of Pratt," I said.

This got a barking laugh. "Now you are wasting my time."

"She told me that she was going to keep it from you. You ruined her mission, and she was going to ruin yours." I knew it would make him angry. But I also hoped it would make him pause to consider it. It did. For less than two seconds.

His hand with the knife tensed again. I forced myself not to close my eye. It would only slice my eyelid. He pulled his hand back. Nachash whispered for me to be brave like he had when I first came to him as a kid. And then the lights went out. The power that kept the restraints in place went with them. I pulled my hands free and slid down in one motion. The knife plunged into the chair above me. Pratt had gotten my message.

I freed my legs and drove my knee into the Suit's groin. It doubled him over, but he recovered quickly. He wasn't Nachash, but he was good. I pulled his gun from his shoulder holster. He knocked it free, sending it sliding across the floor.

The lights went back on. I lunged for the table with the interrogation tools, but it took my eyes precious seconds to adjust to normal light. The Suit knew the room better than I did. He got there first. He grabbed a thirteen-inch spiral blade dagger and thrust it at my gut.

I spun away and backpedaled to gain space. I unbuckled my belt and pulled it free. The Suit closed. I wrapped the belt around my hand in time to deflect another knife thrust and sent a hammer blow to his solar plexus in the same motion. He pivoted, took the punch in the side of his ribs, and raked my chest with the tip of his blade. It wasn't a deep cut, but it hurt plenty.

"I will still cut you piece by piece, but this way it will be sport," he said.

"Did I mention how much I enjoyed fucking your wife? How did you let her get away?"

I slid the belt buckle off my belt as I taunted him. He lunged at me. I set my feet and prepared to deflect a knife thrust to the gut. It was a fake. As soon as I was back on my heels, he threw the knife. I judged the rotation. It would have impaled me through the neck. I got the hand with the belt up just in time to deflect it. The tip cut through to the knuckle. He might manage death by a thousand cuts after all.

I reached for the knife, and he was on me. His hands wrapped around my neck. I shot my hands up between his arms and pushed outward trying to break his grip. The belt buckle was in one of my hands. The belt was wrapped around the other. If I could get the buckle set up to shoot before he strangled me, I had him.

My vision started to go black. I had no choice. I dropped the buckle and grabbed his wrists. I hit the pressure points below where the hand meets the wrist. His grip released, and I twisted away.

He rolled toward the knife. I hit him in the kidney. He flinched but still managed to get to the knife. I slid backward and scooped up the belt buckle as I regained my feet. I made a move toward the table of interrogation tools. The Suit cut me off. He tacked toward me, herding me toward a corner.

It was interesting that he didn't call Caroline for help. Had I put enough doubt in his mind that he didn't trust her or was it pride, wanting to show he could finish me himself?

I unfurled my belt and swung it like a whip to keep him at bay. Setting up the buckle was hard to do with one hand. I would have to try to modify its design if I lived through this.

I let him corner me. I needed him to get close if my buckle gun was going to be effective. I only had one shot. I had to make sure it didn't just wound him.

"Look at the two of us? Fighting to the death over a piece of software. My father fought Arabs for the safety of his home. How did it come to this?" he said, trying to lull me in preparation for his charge.

I hadn't gotten the buckle set yet. "Old war horses. New times. I'm sorry about your partner. I never like to kill a fellow pro."

"We don't choose the job. The job chooses us. It is only a matter of time. For all of us." He rushed toward me, knife extended.

He was quicker than I expected. He had saved an extra gear to finish me. I snapped the buckle in place. He stabbed upward trying to slice under my ribs and into my heart. I chopped down hard with my belt hand across his wrist. With the other hand I brought the buckle gun up to his forehead.

I felt the knife slice through my skin. I pulled the trigger on the buckle gun. Blood spurted from my abdomen. A small red dot appeared on the Suit's forehead. I saw the look of surprise on his face. He fell backward leaving the knife in my gut. How far had it penetrated? The med school student in me tried to assess if it had hit any vital organs, calculated how much blood I would lose, guessed how much time I had left to live. I needed to call for help before I lost consciousness. Would Caroline help me if I did? And then it was too late.

CHAPTER FOURTEEN

dreamed that I was a little boy visiting my father's office. Mrs. Levine was giving me her, "Why do you always show up at the worst times" glare. The patients in the waiting room were trying to disguise their stares, curious what the doctor's kid looked like. And I thought how cool it was that they were all there to see my dad. He was going to make them better. It was a time before his distance and disappointment had overcome my hero worship. Was this heaven? It wasn't where I thought I was ticketed to go. Maybe it was hell, caught forever in the fantasies of my youth knowing how misguided they would prove to be.

Then I was back in the interrogation chair. The bright lights made my head hurt. But now it was my father's voice that asked the questions. Maybe this was hell.

"Can you hear me, Gibbons? Squeeze my finger if you can hear me."

The lights belonged to my father's examining room and my hand was indeed wrapped around his finger. It was the way I used to hold his hand when I was a toddler, my tiny hand wrapped around one of his strong fingers. Now his finger felt small in my hand. His skin was drier than I remembered. I squeezed to see if I could.

"That's good, Gibbons. You lost a great deal of blood, but you're going to be okay. It would have been much easier if your friend Caroline hadn't forbade me to take you to the hospital, of course."

This wasn't hell, but my stomach hurt like it. And my father looked more ragged than I had ever seen him. He had some stubble across his cheeks and chin. I couldn't remember the last time he was anything but clean-shaven.

"How long have I been out?"

"Sixty hours or so," he said.

"And you've been here the whole time?"

"Where else would I be?"

He hadn't left my bedside. Was that a father's love or the diligent doctor? I felt bad for wondering.

"Caroline?"

"She said to give you this."

He fished around in his pocket and pulled out a tiny metallic circle. It was the tracking microdot I had placed on Pratt's computer. I laughed and felt like my stomach was going to fly out through my mouth.

"She also left a backpack full of some unusual items. A gun, a bulletproof vest, a computer, a cell phone, among various other sundries. She asked if you would hold them for her," he said.

"Caroline is helping me with research for my Moron books. She works in counterterrorism. She let me come along with her on what were supposed to be routine surveillance missions, and things didn't go the way they were expected to. That's all I can say."

My father nodded as if I'd told him that I'd been injured in a fender bender. "I suggest that you don't mention any of this to your mother. I told her I gave you an appendectomy. She's a bit of a worrier."

"Why tell her anything?"

"Because she's going to wonder why your abdomen is bandaged when I bring you home."

"Home with you?"

"Caroline made it clear that you could not be admitted to a hospital, given the nature of her work. And I don't plan on spending another night here watching you."

"I have a home of my own. I'm perfectly capable of taking care of myself."

"As a matter of fact you're not. You were lucky that no internal organs were damaged, but you're weak from loss of blood and you're not out of danger of infection."

"I'll stay with Suzanne," I lied.

"I called Suzanne. She was, shall we say, very amenable to our caring for you."

"I'll have a friend stay with me," I said.

"Who?"

"Connor. My editor. He's a great guy. He'll take good care of me." It was pathetic that I couldn't come up with a single real friend.

"You'll stay with us until you are out of danger. After that you can do as you please. The alternative is that I will call an ambulance and certify that you're delirious and need to be forcibly admitted." My father stared me down, daring me to test him. If he had been the Suit, I would have shot him, but he was my father, so I lost. I hated to put my parents in danger, but assuming Westfield hadn't cracked my identity yet, they should be safe. And he didn't leave me any choice. I fully believed he would call the ambulance.

He helped me out to the parking lot. My Camry was parked next to his Mercedes. He drove me home at exactly the speed limit. My mother was waiting in the dining room for us with a full meal set out on the table.

"You know Gibbons can't eat solid food yet," was my father's loving greeting to her.

My mother pulled out a blender full of viscous orange liquid. "I have Gibbons's meal right here," she said. "Carrot juice with strained fruit." I gave her immense credit for keeping a note of triumph out of her voice. My father gave her the smallest of nods.

We sat down at the table as we used to when I still lived in this strange alternate universe. My father was at the head. My mother was to his right, and I was to his left. It hurt to sit up, but I wasn't going to let my father see that. I sipped my orange dinner and thought that it was appropriate that I was back in my childhood home eating something that resembled baby food.

"How is your writing coming?" my mother asked as if I were working on the Great American Novel.

"Books that actually have 'moron' in the title can't be called writing. They're more like violent comic books," my father replied as if I were distributing porn.

And that's how the dinner went. My mother asked the most innocuous questions, and my father turned them into barbed wire. I wondered if they did this when they were alone or if I was the one who brought out this strange duet. How did Devon feel during all the dinners that Suzanne and I bickered through?

After dinner, my mother escorted me up to my old bedroom and tucked me in. She sat on the side of the bed like she used to and waited for me to tell her what was on my mind. She had great patience, honed from years of living with my father. Or perhaps she had the patience from the start, and that was why she had been able to marry my father to begin with.

"I'm sorry I haven't called as much as I should. It's been a bit hectic," I said.

"I know. Suzanne told me that Devon's been having some problems."

Did everyone talk to Suzanne more than I did? "He's too mature in some ways and still a little kid in others. But he'll work it out. He has such a good heart. He'll find his way."

"That's exactly how I felt about you," she said.

"How did you end up taking me to Nachash?" The question came out seemingly of its own accord.

"The school psychologist suggested it. You were having some trouble with the other kids. She said Nachash had worked with a few children in the area and heard that he had been very helpful."

It was a classic recruiting technique. You keep an eye out for troubled kids you could mold. That doesn't mean that's what it was. Maybe Nachash really did get his Zen off by helping kids.

"I didn't approve of all the fighting, but he told me that you were a special boy and that all you needed was a little confidence. And he was right," my mother added.

I wondered if she offered unconditional approval to balance my father's unconditional disapproval? No, that wasn't fair to her. She had a heart that gave itself without question. How else could she love my father for all these years?

"Are you okay, Mom? I know it's not easy with Dad sometimes."

"He's hard on you, Gib, and I'm sorry for that. He doesn't know how to tell you how much he loves you. That's who he is. But your father takes good care of me. You never have to worry about that," she said.

I levered myself up and kissed her on the forehead. It cost me a slash of pain across my gut, but it was worth it.

"It's good to have you home, dear. I'm sorry it's because you're not feeling well, but it's a treat to have you with us," she said.

I knew she meant it. Maybe she meant it enough for both of them. I washed down two Vicodin that my father had reluctantly given me. He was old school. He thought Tylenol was enough for any injury. I almost didn't give him the satisfaction of asking, but my gut convinced me otherwise. I drifted off to sleep and dreamed of Caroline. We were high school versions of ourselves making out in the bed I was sleeping in. A cold draft woke me. And in my groggy state I thought I saw Caroline come through the bedroom window.

"Nice room. Do they keep it as a shrine to your arrested adolescence?" she asked.

I looked around the room and registered for the first time that it was almost untouched since my high school days. Movie posters, record collection, the all-in-one stereo system that had seemed state-of-the-art, they were all here.

"This is actually my father's room, he's letting me sleep here," I said.

"Your father was never an adolescent. He was born an adult."

"Don't make me laugh. It hurts."

"You see what happens when I'm not there to take a bullet for you?"

"You *were* there."

"Nice move with the message to Pratt. You're sorry you left him in the dark and apologizing for being inferior. He remembered what you had told him at that pet shop word for word," she said.

"Did you figure it out before or after you gave him the message?"

"What's your guess?" she said.

"It would have been easier if you had shot your ex yourself."

"Why would I do that?" she said.

"He kills me and you can rat him out to his superiors for killing an American agent in cold blood and end his career. I kill him and you're rid of him for good. You're scary."

"Or maybe I saved your life again," she said.

"So you're either ice cold or warm and fuzzy, and I'll never know."

"I could try to convince you." She climbed on top of me and gave me a long slow kiss. It would have made me melt if my gut wasn't on fire. I tried not to let on.

"It's okay. We'll take a rain check," she said and snuggled in beside me.

"Your gear is in the closet. You don't need to go through the motions."

"I'm not. I feel comfortable with you," she said.

"Irresistibly sexy would be a better compliment."

"In our work you have to be too many different people. Feeling comfortable to be yourself, that's rare."

"You barely know me."

"If you're good at this job, you size people up quickly. I know who you are."

"And who is that?" I said.

"A good person who wants to do the right thing and is finding it harder and harder to figure out what that is."

"It's the thought that counts?" I said.

"Intentions matter. We try to do good things and we can't help doing bad things. When you can no longer tell the difference, that's when you're in trouble."

"Or you can tell the difference and you don't care," I said.

"Even worse."

"It's okay to do terrible things as long as you mean well? That's a little easy, isn't it?" I said.

"No, it isn't. It isn't at all," she said.

Curled up in a ball in my narrow high school bed, she seemed almost vulnerable. "I'm guessing you didn't come here to cheer me up. What do you need?"

"I have a plan."

It was one time I was absolutely sure I believed her. She always had a plan.

· · · · · · · · · ·

I spent a little over forty-eight hours at my parents' house and almost lost my mind. I spent most of the time looking at the webcams at the Big House. I was trapped in the past and I watched as my future went on without me. And worse, I couldn't be there to protect them.

Caroline had assured me that Pratt and the boys were still doing everything they could to keep my identity a secret, but as good as they were, they couldn't erase every trace I'd ever left, and sooner or later Westfield would find one. The only saving grace was that I didn't see Rowan around.

By the second morning, I was determined to leave. My mother brought breakfast up to me as I was getting dressed. She had been bringing me three meals a day and trying to push snacks on me in between. My father had prescribed bed rest, and my mother was every bit as determined as Mrs. Levine when it came to following his directions. "Your father said you'd try to leave. He asked that you wait for him to see you at lunch."

"Since when does Dad come home for lunch?" My father wolfed a brown bag lunch my mother packed and got back to his patients. That was his routine.

"He can't work the same hours anymore. He's not as young as he used to be."

The thought of my father as anything other than a human-like indestructible machine was hard for me to digest. I almost suggested that she check his fuel rods. "Please tell him I'll take a rain check for lunch."

"He said you'd say that, too. He has to at least change your dressing. He'll be here at one."

I couldn't leave my mother to the mercy of my father's disappointment, which he had counted on. At exactly one, I heard his measured tread up the stairs to my room. He got right to business. "You were always a fast healer," he said as he examined the wound. "But be careful. You won't be full strength for a while yet."

"I'll be fine. It's hard to hurt yourself writing."

"Gibbons, am I a smart man?"

"I'm going to assume that's rhetorical," I said.

"Given the nature of your injury, the scars from past wounds, your muscle tone, not to mention your new companion, I can be fairly certain that whatever you're involved in does not involve penmanship."

"I'm sorry to disappoint you, as usual."

"I'm not disappointed. I'm frightened. I knew no son of mine would waste his career on those guidebooks for martial masturbation. If you didn't want to share what you were doing, it was none of my business, but your work is clearly dangerous and your ability to defend yourself is severely impaired."

My father actually felt concern for my welfare. It was wrapped in his usual mix of pride and egocentricity, but it was there nonetheless.

"It's not that I don't want to tell you. I can't. Staying here puts you and Mom at risk. And I can't do that any longer."

"Tell me one thing," he said, as he bandaged me up. "Are you good at what you do?"

"One of the best."

He nodded to himself and handed me a bag full of antibiotics and pain meds. "Take care of yourself, Gibbons. It would kill your mother if something happened to you."

"But you'd get over it."

"Someone would have to take care of her."

How could I argue with his logic? I hugged him before I left. I don't know if I did it because I wanted to or to see what he would do. He hugged me back.

. . . .

I parked in town and came at my house from the side. I wanted to be able to see the back and the front from a single vantage point. The front door and the bay window in the back were the easiest points of entry. That's where any surveillance would be looking. That didn't mean they wouldn't have eyes on the sides of the house as well, but they would definitely watch the front and back.

Half a block away from my house, one of the neighbors had built a tree house. Their sons were long grown, and it provided perfect visibility. With my binoculars, I could also see into a lot of my neighbors' windows, which made me wonder if the parents who built the tree house hadn't inadvertently turned their boys into Peeping Toms.

My watch-and-wait took me through the afternoon and into the evening. I needed to observe the scene in daylight and after dark. I munched on Triscuits and Brie that my mother had forced on me and drank from a Thermos of tea she had prepared. My gut felt like it had been stitched with barbed wire, but I didn't want to take a painkiller and dull my senses.

By midnight, I was convinced that I was clear. I made my way quickly and quietly to the house. I checked the windows front and back and on the opposite side of the house to make sure there was no one hiding inside. I didn't trust my webcams.

I checked the basement where I had state-of-the-art bug jammers set up. They seemed to be working normally. I searched the rest of the house to make sure I was alone, turned on the security system, took two Vicodin, and went to sleep.

I woke up to the phone ringing. I looked at the caller ID and saw it was Suzanne's cell. It was already into the school day for her. Had someone grabbed her and was using her phone?

"Are you okay?" was my greeting.

"You're the one who had surgery," she said.

It took me a second to remember that I supposedly had an appendectomy. "I'm fine. You don't usually call during school time."

"I need to talk to you, and I don't want to do it with Devon in the house. Can you meet me after school?"

"Is Devon okay?"

"Yes, we are all okay, Gib. I just need to talk to you. Can you be at the house at 1:30?"

"Sure. Should I bring Taco Bell?"

She didn't laugh even a little, which was a good sign that she was okay and not being coerced. I approached the Big House, the same way I had approached mine. I showed up early and watched. By the time Suzanne came home, I was pretty sure no one was on us. I stashed my gear in the Camry, waited a few minutes, and rang the bell. Suzanne was dressed in her work clothes. She was the cool preschool teacher who wore jeans and a black turtleneck. I always liked her in that look. It wasn't trying too hard.

I followed her into the kitchen. Neither of us were coffee drinkers. She had teacups out and a plate of Oreos. Green tea and cookies, it was our version of high tea. Suzanne was not only a vegetarian, she was big on whole, healthy foods. She limited Devon's junk food consumption, but she had a secret sugar addiction. I sipped my tea and waited for her to talk. It took her a while to warm up when she had something important to say.

"Dean broke up with me. Out of the blue. Do you have any idea why?" I had some thoughts. I tried not to look too happy.

"He said that there was still too much going on with you and me. Why would he say that?"

"He's not as dumb as he looks?" I said.

"I asked him if you had talked to him, and he looked scared. Did you threaten him in some way?"

"As much as I'd like to take credit, what could I possibly say that would scare Rowan?"

"Dean can be a little full of himself, but he's not a bad guy. He was considerate, he was honest, and he was there. I don't understand what would suddenly make him end things," she said.

"I won't pretend I like the guy, but I'm sorry it hurt you."

"And you had nothing to do with it?"

"Of course not. And part of the reason you're upset is because he picked up on something you don't want to admit. There are still strong feelings between us."

She got up out of her chair and I braced for a slap. Suzanne had a pretty tight hold on her temper, but in the rare instances that it broke free, she could be pretty fierce. What I wasn't prepared for was a kiss. It felt new and familiar at the same time. It wasn't the electric jolt I got from Caroline. It took me deeper and more completely. We undressed each other with urgency. We knew what lay beneath and rushed into its familiar embrace. We had never made love on the kitchen floor when we were married. It always felt cliché. And cold linoleum is not exactly an aphrodisiac, but it didn't matter. We found the best of rediscovery, and the cold didn't register as we lay panting afterward in each other's arms.

"I had a lot of feelings good and bad toward you and I guess they needed to come out," she said.

"I am always here to help."

Her elbow to the ribs sent pain shooting all the way down to my feet. I could have blocked it, but launching a Krav Maga counterattack on your ex-wife tended to be bad for your cover and your relationship.

"I'm sorry. I forgot you're still recovering."

"I will never recover," I said.

"That makes you sound like the victim and that's not fair."

"I am a victim, of my own making. But I never wanted to make you one, you or Devon," I said.

"You're a good father, a little deluded sometimes, but I know that's out of love."

"But not a good husband," I said.

"It's funny, I think about that a lot. It's not like you were ever mean or that you neglected me. It's just that you weren't *all* there. There was some part of you that you wouldn't share. And I thought I could live with that. But it started to drive me crazy. And finally I realized I deserved all of you and I couldn't settle for less."

"You did have all of me. You still do," I said.

"You couldn't even tell me the truth about that blonde woman you were with."

"We're working together and that is absolutely the truth."

She looked at me for a long moment. "I believe you. And I still feel like there's more you're not telling me."

This was why it was impossible for contractors to stay married. The more your spouse got to know you, the more they could tell when you were lying. And you could never tell them the whole truth. "I love you, Suzanne. There is no one else. There never has been."

"And as much as I like to hear that, you still didn't answer my question."

"It's funny, I thought I did."

"Maybe that's the problem. It's not that we can't find the right answers. We're asking different questions," she said.

"That sounds like something that could be worked out," I said.

"I don't know, Gib. I don't know if I have the energy to try again."

"Then I'll make it easy for you. Agree to dinner tonight. You don't need much energy for dinner. We can go to that new Mediterranean place that opened in town. It's all vegetarian."

"You're going to give up meat for a night? Now I know you love me," she said.

"I'll pick you up at seven."

"Gib . . ."

"I'm coming here at seven, either way. Don't make me grovel in front of our son," I said.

"If you're going to grovel, beg him to do his homework."

"I thought that he was better about that now."

"He says he is, but he still spends all his time in his room with the door closed."

It was domestic talk after sex as only married couples share. There was a time when I had wished for sexier post coital banter, but now I realized I missed it. Devon was a bond only the two of us shared.

"Maybe he's jerking off," I said.

"I wish it were that simple."

"I could advise him. I'm very good at it."

"Oh, is that what you're good at," she said.

"Not the only thing." I kissed her on the neck. She always loved to be kissed on the neck. She laughed and squirmed away.

"I have to take a shower and get ready to pick up Devon."

"Let me pick him up," I said.

"So you can advise him?"

"So I can spend time with him. And with you."

She stopped squirming away and started squirming in the right way.